INVADE HELL

# MEPHITIC

*ANATHEMA — BOOK TWO*

*YOLANDA OLSON*

*JENNIFER BENE*

ISBN (e-book): 978-1-946722-70-6

ISBN (paperback): 978-1-946722-71-3

Cover design by Dez Purington, http://prettyininkcreations.com/

 Created with Vellum

## Anathema Series

Noxious

Mephitic

Viperous

## The Wannabe

The best and worst idea I've ever had blew up in my face big time.

Willa and Dexter are gone; traded away for the worst man I've ever met in my life and the most obsessive little fiend that would sooner die than not have his full attention.

I'm on the road again, but it's nowhere I want to be.

I don't even know where the destination is exactly. All I do know is that I'd rather be anywhere than here or there.

My friends…

I'm sorry.

## The Replacement

I thought my luck had run out on the curb of a rest area somewhere in Pennsylvania.

I've never been so wrong.

Someone found me, tucked me under his arm, and promised me a great time—and for the most part, I suffered one disappointment after the other.

Until him.

He sees me, knows me in ways that I don't even know myself, and when he smiles at me…

I'll never let him go.

---

**The Fury**

If it's not the emo kids at the stupid church, it's something else.

I spent most of my time happy at home with nothing but my … friend … to pass the time.

That was all I ever thought I needed to be honest, and I know damn well, it's all he's needed. I mean anyone that comes into my crosshairs usually knows they're in for a time as magnificent as the sight they're beholding, and I like to do my best to show them that.

Of course, that's not to say that I don't like to have my own fun.

In my special ways, that is.

But now I've got the chance to show up at the doorstep of someone that's haunted me for longer than I care to admit.

What's one more road trip to the pits of hell to see this through to the end.

Am I right?

## ONE

## He Always Knew

ICHABOD

"What?"

The sound of shock in my voice is enough to draw Lakyn's attention away from Aftyn. He gives me a sidelong glance, the grin growing tight on his lips before he runs a hand back through his hair and shrugs.

"What?" he echoes, his eyes becoming hard and stern. His visage tells me that he doesn't think this is the time for me to be brave, but I know him better than he knows himself—and having me stand up to him usually puts him in a good, yet dangerous mood.

"You told me you didn't know where Bea was. Every time I've asked you, you said you never kept track of her," I accuse in a shaky tone.

I'm sure I resemble Aftyn when he first saw Lakyn's face. Fists balled at my sides, shaking from slight anger, and wondering what Lakyn's next move will be.

"Nooooo," Lakyn corrects with a smile. "I said that I didn't *care.* Big difference."

Damn near twenty years spent being his whipping boy, and I'm not entirely sure why I'm so shocked right now. Lakyn Meyer has never been one to tell a lie—it's something he abhors, but it sure as fuck has never stopped him from bending the truth to suit his needs.

"So, where is she?" I bark at him.

The room falls silent as Lakyn makes a show of sidestepping to stand right in front of me. He tilts his head to the side and looks me straight in the eyes. Usually that's enough to unnerve me, but not this time.

Not when Bea's whereabouts are on the line.

"Well?" I press as bravely as I can.

Lakyn rolls his eyes as he glances at his son, then the two girls behind him, before he shrugs and goes back to his seat. "See what you guys did? Now this one is gonna be bitching at me for the rest of my life."

A dramatic sigh escapes him as he leans back in the chair and turns his face toward the ceiling. It's almost like he's experiencing some kind of cosmic blowjob, but if he thinks that letting this piece of news slip is going to make me feel frisky, he's got another thing coming.

"Anyway," he continues as he sits upright again and rolls his shoulders. His eyes go back to Aftyn. "What do you say? Wanna meet your auntie?"

Aftyn sniffles next to me and I reach over to put a reassuring hand on his shoulder. Lakyn likes to keep his secrets, but at the very least, this one should be acknowledged more than just the lame joke I tried for a reaction.

"Hey," Lakyn barks. I glance over at him and he shakes his head. *Ever the control freak,* I think as I square my jaw.

But I don't drop my hand, if anything I give Aftyn's shoulder a squeeze and when he turns his eyes toward me, I motion with my head for him to sit with me on the couch, which he does.

Once we're comfortable I put my hands on my knees and lean forward, my eyes on the man that's used me and abused me for more than half of my life and I clench my teeth.

Beatrix St. Germain has been my best friend since she found me digging through some dumpsters to feed my family. I was fifteen years old, hungry, tired, and unaware of the real evil that hides in the world... and she did her best to keep me safe from it.

Her best wasn't good enough, though. Even so, I never really had an unkind thing to say about her. If anything, I always wanted to be the reason she smiled, felt happy and safe, and maybe one day even loved.

But the bastard in front of me has always been the opposite of Beatrix's good qualities and when our adventures were over, I found out that she was worse than him.

She bartered me.

A payment to Lakyn for helping her reach her ascension, and I've been nothing more than a piece of meat to be tenderized and fucked mercilessly ever sense.

Still.

I can't help but wish that he'd love me.

Even just a little bit.

I rub my face with my hands irritably.

I know that I'll never be anything more than the dutiful pup that wants to please his owner at every turn. Any time that I try to grow a pair and stand up to him, it never works.

Ever.

This time has to be different, though.

He's held something from me that I've been desperate to know, to touch, to *feel* again, and I want answers.

"Why wouldn't you tell me?" I ask him in a softer tone. Not that soft or gentle are things that Lakyn understands, but anything is worth a shot right now.

"Because that's a boring subject," he replies with a shrug.

I shake my head as I throw myself back against the couch cushions and blow out a breath. He's not going to tell me a goddamn thing about where Beatrix is and I'm going to have to grovel to go with them, but I'll be good and goddammned if he thinks I'm staying behind now.

"Um, excuse me?"

I angle my head so that I can see the little blonde who's been watching our exchange curiously. All eyes in the room are on her now and she looks as nervous as Lakyn looks bored.

"Something to say?" he asks her, feigning curiosity.

"I was just wondering," she begins slowly as she pushes her hair behind her ears. "Does he live here too?

She nods in my direction and I can see Lakyn stiffen slightly.

Ah, the one chord he hates having struck has been plucked in a room full of strangers and I know this isn't going to end well.

"Not that it's any of your fucking business, but yeah. Why?" he snarls at her, his eyes narrowing.

In my head, I can already hear the music playing. Lakyn likes to crank his favorite tunes while he tortures, kills, fucks, whatever he's in the mood to do to get him off, and her asking a question so innocent has flipped his switch on.

"We're roommates," I offer, hoping to save her from the hell she's just swan-dived into.

She arches an eyebrow curiously at me before she turns her attention slowly toward Aftyn, who stiffens next to me. I smile despite myself. *Just like his father.*

"Weird. The way you two just went back and forth, I was so sure that maybe you were his stepdaddy," she says with a smirk and a nod at Aftyn.

My eyes immediately cut to Lakyn who's grinding his teeth. I can see the movement through his jaw, and I know there's no saving anyone in this room now.

It just depends on whose blood he wants to have rush over his hands.

## TWO

## The Second Coming

LAKYN

I've never been one to give a shit about what other people do in their homes, or wherever the hell they do it, which includes the gay ones. This world is a mess most days, and whatever it takes to snag a piece of happiness for yourself—I say go for it. Personally, I've always been a fan of blasting the best songs of the eighties, seeing how creative I can be while I make a chick scream, and whether I give her the privilege of feeling my dick before she dies, or if I use Ichabod after the fun is over, it doesn't really matter.

It's my little slice of sunshine and happiness, and I got Ichabod fair and square. But the little blonde bitch on the couch thinks she's got me all figured out, like she has a fucking clue why Ichabod is in this house.

Not that I plan on explaining myself to her.

I hold onto the smile and stare at her until she starts to squirm, the smirk on her face wobbling for a second before it collapses completely. Then she clears her throat and looks over at the kid. "Aftyn, you've had your little family reunion. We should go."

"Be quiet," Aftyn hisses at her, and I chuckle and shift my gaze to Ichabod—who's still testing out his recently descended balls. He's pissed at me, but it's just because he's always had a hard-on for Trixie. I don't know why he won't just let the little satanic psycho go. She handed him over to me so she could be Satan's number one bitch, and it's not like I've changed my fucking address. If she really wanted to be Ichabod's savior or whatever, she's had plenty of time to show up.

Not that I would have let her take him, but I probably could have convinced her to bend over for me before I kicked her the fuck out.

Ichabod sighs and looks to the side, watching the blonde and the boy whispering at each other. It's annoying, and since I'm obviously not getting a strip tease out of the kid, then it's time to move to my back-up entertainment for the evening. Grabbing my cigarettes, I take another one out and light it, blowing a cloud of smoke toward the ceiling before I look at the last unwanted guest on the couch.

The redhead isn't paying attention to the irritating whispers beside her. Nope, she's got her eyes on me and I can tell she likes what she sees. But, who doesn't? I turn on my charming smile and lean forward, bracing my elbows on my knees, and the way she smiles back tells me that I might still have one potential member of the Cult of Lakyn.

I just don't know if she's worth the time or not.

"Hey, Red," I say, and she sits up a little straighter. So happy to be called on. "Since we're doing this whole family reunion thing... you wanna be part of the family?"

"What?" the blonde snaps, turning to scoff at the redhead, and I see the same flicker of rage on Red's face that I saw outside. "This is ridi—"

"Yes," Red answers, eyes on me, exactly like they should be.

"Good. There's just one problem." Leaning back in the chair, I take another drag on my cigarette before I point it at the two young girls on the couch. "There's not enough room for everyone in the car," I continue, keeping my voice nonchalant as I meet Red's gaze. "Show me how bad you want it."

The redhead's smile spreads, and I'm not sure what I expected from her, but when she turns, unzips her backpack, and pulls out a knife, I let out a laugh.

"Shit!" the blonde shouts, jumping up from the couch. She almost falls over the coffee table but manages to move around it as Red rises much more calmly.

"What the fuck!" Aftyn shouts, but Ichabod grabs hold of the kid, yanking him back onto the couch before he looks at me. If Ichabod thinks I'm kidding, he might want to turn that sad puppy stare on the redhead currently facing off with the blonde in the middle of the living room. This chick is full of surprises, and I have to admit she reminds me a little bit of Trixie as she adjusts her hold on the knife, looking damn happy about it.

"Lakyn…" Ichabod says my name quietly, and I grin at him for a second, not wanting to miss a thing.

"Just enjoy the show. You don't want me bored, right?" I ask, and he snaps his mouth shut, holding tight to Aftyn as I turn back at the girls. "You two need to get all oiled up first?"

"You call this fair?" the blonde screeches, ignoring my very good suggestion as red just shrugs.

"I told you, I don't give a shit about fair," Red answers with that weird, stiff smile on her face. "I just want to see what you're like when you drop the mask."

I'm about to tell them to stop fucking around when the blonde screams and lunges for Red, grabbing onto her knife hand, but Red cracks her in the face with her elbow. The second the blonde stumbles back to grab her nose, Red buries the knife deep in her stomach and then yanks it upward. The blonde's eyes go wide, and I stand up just to get a better angle. There's so much shock on her face, and I'm glad that at least one piece of entertainment worked out for the evening.

"NO!" the kid shouts, and Ichabod slaps his hand over the boy's mouth, practically climbing in his lap to keep him on the couch. I'd be more interested in what the hell Ichabod thinks he's doing if there wasn't something beautiful happening center stage.

"Death is death, Willa," Red says, and I grin when I realize she's twisting the knife back and forth like she's trying to dig a hole straight through the bitch. The blonde one coughs, spraying blood on Red's chest and shirt, and then she drops to one knee and the knife slides free. Red looks at me as she grabs a handful of the blonde's hair, moving behind her to place the knife at her throat, but I hold up a hand and she freezes.

Chuckling, I crouch down in front of the blonde, listening to the jagged breaths that tell me the fun is almost over since her lungs are quickly filling with blood. *Pity*. She could have been fun in my playroom. Still, crazy Red definitely makes me think of the more fun parts of Trixie, and that brings back a fond memory. "Hey!" I snap my fingers in front of the blonde's face, waiting until she seems vaguely aware of me before I flash a smile. "Say you love Lakyn."

Red shakes her, but the gurgling sound coming from the blonde is a disappointing attempt—if she even fucking tried. Such a waste of space, she didn't even put up a decent enough fight to make the entertainment last a little while. I roll my eyes and stand up, taking another drag on my cigarette as I step back from them, but Red's intense gaze catches my attention. I grin when I realize she's waiting for me like a good little acolyte, and I blow out the smoke before I nod at her.

"I love Lakyn," Red says, her voice all sweet and calm just before she drags the knife across the blonde bitch's throat without her gaze ever leaving mine. Red's got pale gray-brown eyes that hold the same glint of worship I've seen in photos of Manson's followers, and I have to admit it's not bad being worshiped. She's young, pretty, and batshit crazy, which means at a minimum I'll let her come along to meet Trixie. After all, she's obviously got more of a spine than the kid.

"What the FUCK, Daphne!" Aftyn shouts, shoving at Ichabod as he finally breaks free and climbs over the coffee table to drop next to the blonde, but I tilt my head and look at him.

"What did you just call her?" I ask, even though Aftyn is too busy having some kind of *moment* with the corpse of the blonde. Letting out a loud, rolling laugh,

I look up at the redhead and slap my leg with my free hand. "Jinkies! Looks like you won, Daphne!"

Her smile stretches, and I lean to look past her, catching Ichabod's worried gaze. "Why the fuck haven't you ever been able to do that?"

Shaking his head, Ichabod clenches his jaw and gets up from the couch, moving to comfort the kid again. If he thinks I'm going to let him test out the younger model, he's forgetting that I don't like to share my toys. Plus, the kid would probably be too sweet with him, and then I'd have to put up with Ichabod doing a half-hearted job the next time I need to get off, which just isn't acceptable.

"So… I get to come with you?" Daphne asks, and I suck my teeth as I look Ichabod over one more time before facing her again.

"Looks like it," I reply, stretching before I drop back into the chair and tap my cigarette on the ash tray. "Unfortunately, I don't have a dog, and my car isn't called the Mystery Machine."

"Zoinks," Daphne deadpans, and I wag my finger at her, chuckling.

"So, were you named after Scooby and the gang?" I ask, and she shrugs, her eyes still glued to mine like I'm the second coming. And who the fuck knows? Maybe I am.

Glancing over at the corpse on the floor, I take a second to admire her lack of hesitation. When I said jump, Red didn't even bother asking how high—she just went to work, and she already had a knife at the ready. It's been a while since I got to appreciate someone else's work, and it's pretty obvious that this isn't the first time Red has gutted somebody. She's got blood splattered on her cheek and her chest, and the hand still holding the knife is covered in it, but I have a feeling that putting her and Trixie in the same space will be more than a little fun. Just to see if they go for each other's throats or not.

I jerk my chin toward the back of the house. "Go clean yourself up. Bathroom is down the hall. We might as well get on the road."

"I'm coming with you," Ichabod says, standing up to face me, and I grin as he tightens his fists at his sides.

"You really wanna drop your balls today?" I tilt my head, looking down at the bloody mess on the floor. "I thought you wanted to see Beatrix again."

The tension melts off him and I can tell he's thinking about crying. Ichabod has always been too emotional when it comes to that Satan-loving psycho, and I've never understood it, but I figure he might actually go to the mat over this one if I let him think too much.

"Listen, you stay here, clean up this mess." I wave my hand at the dead chick on the floor. "And I'll take the kid to meet his Aunt Trixie. We'll do the family reunion thing, and I'll see if she wants to let you sleep over for a few days."

"You…" Ichabod licks his lips. "You'd let me stay with Bea?" I can tell he doesn't believe me—which would be the smart thing to do. But hope is a bitch. "You'd let me go?"

"Don't get your dick hard for nothing. I said *for a few days*, and that's only if you don't act like a kicked puppy right now. Got it?" Jabbing out the cigarette, I stretch my back and walk over to the couch to drag the hatchet out from under it. If the blonde bitch had been crafty enough, she might have had a chance to defend herself and make the show a little more entertaining, but it's fine. I have a feeling Daphne is going to be plenty of entertainment.

Ichabod nods, helping the kid off the floor, and I ignore their whispers again as Daphne comes back into the living room looking *almost* good as new. Her shirt is a mess, and I point at it.

"Change your shirt, Red." I swing the hatchet up onto my shoulder as she slides the knife back into her backpack and pulls out a clean shirt. When she takes her bloody shirt off in the middle of the living room, I grin and wave a hand at her, glancing over at Ichabod and the kid. "She's not shy, is she?"

Neither of them is paying attention to the half-naked girl, which I expected from Ichabod, but the fact that the kid is still staring at the dead girl instead of the living one just has me rubbing my forehead.

"You sure I stuck my dick in your mom?" I ask and he rounds on me, glaring as I chuckle again. "Just asking, kid."

"Ready," Daphne says cheerfully, pulling the backpack on her shoulders, and I wonder if I picked up a schoolgirl outfit if she'd put it on for the drive. Toss that red hair in pig tails, get some fresh blood spatter on the white button down—it could be fun.

Plenty of ways to avoid boredom on the drive to find Trixie.

Heading past them into the kitchen, I grab a carton of cigarettes from the freezer and a spare lighter from a drawer, tucking the carton under my arm as I move back into the living room and tilt my head toward the front door. "Come on, kid. Let's go."

He's staring at Ichabod, and I snap the fingers on the hand *not* holding the hatchet—which usually keeps people's attention focused squarely on me, as it should be, but doesn't seem to be working as well today.

"Did you know that—" the kid starts to talk, and I groan.

"If you're going to be all chatty the entire drive, this is going to be miserable. Shut up and get outside." Nodding at Red, I go and hold the front door open, snagging my keys and jingling them like I'm trying to get the attention of a pack of rabid toddlers. "Time is ticking."

Ichabod nudges the boy forward, and I grin at him as Red and the kid walk out the front door. He taps one of his shoes on the floor beside the steadily spreading pool of blood, staring down for a moment before he finds his balls again and looks up at me. "Promise me I'll get to see Bea, Lakyn."

"Don't I always keep my word?" I reply, winking at him as I point at the body with the hatchet. "Make sure you handle that, or it's going to suck in here in a day or two."

Slamming the door before Ichabod can start to get emotional over me leaving, I walk out into the sunlight, whistling to myself as I watch the kid dig out a pair of duffel bags from the back of the SUV. I'm about to toss my shit in my car, when I look over at the SUV and grin. Why should I put the miles on my car when the kid has something shiny and new.

Heading across the road, I shove my keys in my pocket and grin when the kid freezes near the open back. "We'll take your car. It's spacious, better for road trips. Keys?"

I hold out my hand and he grinds his teeth for a few seconds, but I'm not above breaking a few of them if it means he won't waste any more of my time. Lucky for him, he digs them out and shoves them into my hand with a muttered phrase I don't bother trying to make out.

"Smart move." Turning on my heel, I hop into the driver's seat and toss my shit inside, making sure the hatchet is within reach in the back floorboard before I tuck my current pack of cigarettes in the visor.

Lighting up, I crank the car on and roll the window down before I start tapping the horn when the kid is taking his sweet time rearranging the bags in the back.

"The devil waits for no one!" I shout over my shoulder and angle the rearview mirror to watch the kid glaring at me just as Daphne starts to get in the backseat. I shake my head and tap the passenger headrest. "Up here. I don't want the kid getting too attached."

She smiles at me as she climbs in the front seat and I know this was the right choice. The kid is just going to glare at me for a while, and I'd much rather be worshiped by the person in my peripheral vision.

Next stop, Satan's doorstep.

## THREE

## Replacements and Resentments

AFTYN

I have my eyes closed and my back so firmly planted in the seat that I could almost swear I'm trying to become one with it.

It smells mostly like Daphne, but like Dexter too. The one scent I never want to lose is the one that belonged to my best friend, Willa, but I know that Lakyn's constant smoking will blot that out just like Daphne did her life.

'*I fed her to the fucking wolves*,' I think miserably, and I feel angry as a tear rolls down my cheek. We loved each other—even if not in the way I knew we could—but in the way that best friends often do.

And I guess karma played her hand earlier than I would have imagined.

I took out Dexter for trying to keep Wills to himself and Daphne killed her to keep Lakyn to herself.

*All because I didn't want to stand down on a dare.*

"Crying again?" The amused, disapproving tone of Lakyn floats back toward me and I open my eyes to meet his in the rearview mirror.

I wipe my sweaty palms against my jeans and clear my throat. He's nothing like I'd hoped he would be. He's cruel, clearly doesn't give two shits about anything other than himself, and maybe Daphne.

*Maybe Mom wasn't so bad after all.*

"My best friend was just murdered in front of me. You'll have to forgive me if—"

Lakyn lets out a loud, fake snoring sound and I grit my teeth when he turns his eyes toward Daphne and smirks.

The urge to lean forward and pull the steering wheel is starting to build inside of me. I doubt that anyone would mourn either of us if I managed to flip the SUV, unless…

"Didn't mean to bore you," I begin in a clipped, conversational tone. "Your boyfriend is a hell of a lot more interesting, anyway."

Lakyn stiffens.

A small smile begins to creep across my lips as he turns his eyes back toward the road and I watch his knuckles turn white. It seems that the great Lakyn

Meyer has a switch that's easily flipped and I think it'll be fun to play with it.

"Ease up on the steering wheel, Pops," I continue breezily. "Wills loved this fucking truck."

*If he wants to be malicious, two can play this fucking game.*

I run my hands back through my hair as I lean over and grab one of Willa's thin hair ties from the center console. Snapping it around my wrist, I decide that its mine now and will keep me and Wills together for as long as I live.

Bringing my wrist to my nose, I inhale the faint scent of Willa's hair, blink back tears, then drop my hand on the empty spot next to me.

Wills should be sitting here with me. We should both be going to meet this Aunt Beatrix person and instead, she's lying dead on Lakyn's living room floor.

"So, listen," Lakyn finally says as he clears his throat and pulls the pack of cigarettes from the visor. Then he reaches over and taps Daphne's thigh, nodding toward the carton of cigarettes and she immediately opens it, handing him a new pack with the most adoring look in her eyes.

*I should have left you on the sidewalk of the fucking rest area where you belonged.*

"I know you think that you're being witty or cute or whatever it is that you're trying to achieve by saying what you just did. The thing is, kid, that cute and witty doesn't work with me. I'd save the bullshit for Beatrix—she's more into pitiful, bullshit little boys than I am."

"Will do, Pops! Besides, it seems like the silent, sneaky, hopeful ones are more your type anyway," I snipe back as cheerfully as I can.

Lakyn lets out a good-natured laugh as he lights his smoke, inhales deeply, then lets it billow out of the corner of his mouth. He glances at me in the rearview again before he shakes his head.

I brace myself for his next barrage of fatherly love, but instead he begins to tap his fingers along the steering wheel and continues driving.

"Ever been to the desert, kid?" he asks, changing the subject.

"Nope, but I bet your boyfriend has," I say with a grin. "He's the reason I'm here in case you were wondering."

"Don't make me turn this car around!" Lakyn warns in a forced cheerful tone. "Isn't that want parents say, or whatever?" he asks, glancing at Daphne.

"Absolutely," she replies with a vigorous nod and I arch an eyebrow when I catch his eyeroll in the rearview as he turns his attention back toward the road in front of him.

I take the opportunity to lean forward and rest my forearms against the back of Daphne's seat to look at him. A grin begins to spread on his lips and it's obvious to me by now that Lakyn revels in the worship of being looked at.

"I got an email one day when I was at home." He's going to listen to my story whether he wants to or not, and I'll prove to him that I'm no fucking liar. "I was browsing the internet, looking for something that I could get for Wills. It wasn't a special occasion or anything, I just liked being able to surprise her every now and then."

"Boring!" Lakyn intercedes as he takes another drag of his smoke. I don't know what comes over me, but I reach over and smack the back of his chair as hard as I can. He lets out a laugh and a grunt. "Sorry, apparently the blonde meant more to you than you're willing to shut the fuck up about, so go ahead. Did you find any good porn while you were surfing the web, by the way?"

"I'm trying to tell you how I became acquainted with your guy, Pops. Let me finish before you try to be so goddamn loving," I spit at him. Lakyn cracks his neck, then nods just once which I assume means that I have his permission. *Like I fucking asked for it.*

"It's okay, Lakyn," Daphne pipes up. "I like boys too."

Lakyn glances at her, his jaw becoming prominent with anger, but instead of replying to her, he looks over at me, then back toward the road.

"I thought I had found the perfect gift for her, so I went to check my bank balance and realized I was a few hundred dollars short of the prize. No big deal though because I knew she'd let me borrow it if I needed it, you know? Anyway, just as I was ready to log off, I decided to go check my email to see if anything worth reading had landed in there when I saw a message that caught my eye. Simplest subject line ever—*I dare you*."

Lakyn rubs his thumb against his forehead before he taps the ashes off the end of his cigarette out the window then clears his throat. At this point, I'm not even sure if he's listening to me anymore, but I don't fucking care.

He ruined my life by not being there, and then again by having Daphne kill Wills, so I think it's only fair to return the favor.

"If you can't tell by now, I opened the email. It contained a few different addresses in Arizona, a tidbit or two about a man that was supposedly my father, and that all-consuming dare in the tagline. I thought, fuck, this could be fun, so I responded. Over the course of a few weeks, the emails remained constant until I was finally able to talk Wills into coming on this fucking road trip. Then the emails turned into text messages, but no matter how hard I tried to turn them into phone calls, your guy wouldn't answer. What's up with that, Pops? How is it that you seem to be so in control of everything, but your boyfriend is able to sneak around behind your back?"

When he doesn't respond right away, I reach over and smack the back of his chair again. Lakyn chuckles as he clicks his tongue against the back of his teeth before he steals a glance at me.

"Were you saying something? I kinda spaced out there."

I throw myself against the backseat angrily and blow out my breath. In my entire life, I never thought I'd hate someone more than Mom.

Seems I was wrong.

"Forget it," I grumble as I cross my arms over my chest and glance out the window. *Eventually you'll have no choice but to fucking listen to every word I say.*

## FOUR

## Seventeen Going on Eighteen

DAPHNE

I'm back in this stupid SUV for the third time, which means I've broken my rule twice in as many days, but I think this time it might actually be worth it. Willa and Aftyn had turned out to be… disappointing. They'd showed so much promise in the forest, and I'd really thought that laying all our cards on the table would make them more interesting—but no.

Aftyn's dad though? Definitely interesting.

From the first moment I saw him walking across the road I'd felt some kind of pull toward him. An incomprehensible tug that had actually managed to drag my attention away from Willa's bitchy little threats. I'll admit I was lucky that she was just as caught off-guard by the man's loud voice and wide grin and didn't take the opportunity to kill me when she had it, although it's not like she was smart enough to carry a weapon anyway.

But with Lakyn staring at us, none of that had even crossed my mind.

I'd recognized the similarities to Aftyn immediately, but Lakyn has a more refined version of Aftyn's good looks. He's taller, more confident, and even in the casual clothes he seemed to take up more space than his physical body. I won't deny being physically attracted to Aftyn but looking between the two of them the difference between boys and men has never been so clear to me. Lakyn is what Aftyn *could* be if he didn't spend so much time trying to one-up Willa… not that she's a problem anymore. But I still don't think he's going to get any better.

There's just too much emotion in him, and Lakyn can see it too.

Just like Lakyn saw me.

*He asked me if I wanted to be a part of the family.*

Those are the words I never thought I'd hear. Sixteen years of foster homes where I was too weird, too creepy, too quiet and distant and strange… but Lakyn saw right through all of that. When he looked at me, I knew I didn't need to pretend. I didn't have to act like the vulnerable lost girl, because he saw the truth in those first few moments out on the street and he liked it. He invited me in, and then gave me permission to kill Willa with a kind of excitement in his incredible blue eyes that I've never seen in another person.

'*Show me how bad you want it.*' he'd said.

She didn't stand a chance.

Not with joining Lakyn's family on the line. It was the first time I've ever *wanted* to be accepted by anyone, to show them the real me without any plan to kill them after. Willa was too easy to bait, too easy to kill. Yet the way he got out of his chair to get a closer look at what I'd done, wearing a smile and not an ounce of judgment or horror on his face, that felt like a dream come true. He wasn't disgusted. If anything, he looked fascinated as he stared at Willa—but I wanted him to look at me.

I dug the knife in deeper, twisting it to end her faster and regain his attention, and as his lips spread into a grin, I felt the closest to happy I've ever been.

When Willa finally collapsed, I held her upright so I could kill her while facing him. All I'd wanted was for his gaze to meet mine again, but he'd crouched down in front of her and tried to get her attention, tried to make her say she loved him… and I'd realized that was the feeling buzzing in my chest. I *wanted* to be around him. I *wanted* to join his family, to go with him to meet Aftyn's aunt, or wherever the fuck he wanted to take me.

Willa didn't have the capacity to say it, and I think even if I hadn't dragged the knife through her diaphragm she probably would have ruined the moment with some bitchy little comment, so I was glad she just gurgled and choked while I waited for Lakyn to look at me again.

A cloud of smoke left his lips and then his blue eyes met mine, and he nodded. It was a moment of perfect acceptance. Approval. Acknowledgement of the real me... and there was only one response to that.

*I love Lakyn.*

As I slit her throat, his slow grin became the center of my universe for a moment, and I ignored all the shouting and the chaos whirling around us because none of it mattered. I just dropped Willa to the floor and waited to see if I'd done what he'd hoped for. Seventeen years old and I already knew my future belonged to him. The only other person I'd ever met that was like me, that understood me, that *liked* me.

He'd cracked jokes about my name, nothing I haven't heard before. Scooby Doo has been around since before I was born and will probably still be around after I'm dead. That mutt is one of those timeless things in culture, but I'd learned to brush off the comments when I was still a kid, and it paid off because now I'm in the front seat with him, watching him drive while Aftyn mourns his dead friend in the backseat. I don't know why Aftyn doesn't see what's right in front of him. Being related to Lakyn is a gift in his otherwise mediocre life. How many people get to have a connection to someone so vibrant? So unapologetically themselves?

If he'd stop pouting long enough to pay attention, he might actually learn something.

"Want one?" Lakyn asks, his eyes on the road, but he's offering me the last cigarette in his previous pack and I take it. He crushes the pack in his fist and tosses it over his shoulder, chuckling under his breath when Aftyn curses.

"Nice one, Pops." Aftyn huffs, and I glance back to see him pulling his cigarettes out as well. *He* never offered me one, even though the only reason I was ever in this car was because he picked me up off the curb and dragged me with him into the boring dynamic of his relationship with Willa. That's just one more way Lakyn is better than him though.

The lighter is in the cup holder, and though I haven't smoked much, I know how to do it. I crack my window and light it, taking a short puff the first time just to avoid coughing and embarrassing myself. A few drags in and I get that tingly rush from the nicotine. It makes my head swim a little and I lean against the window, adjusting my backpack on my lap so I'm more comfortable as I watch Lakyn drive. "Thank you."

He just nods, letting a billow of smoke out of the corner of his mouth, and I let the road noise fill the silence for a few minutes.

The urge to speak to him again bubbles up inside my chest, and it's such a foreign sensation that I don't know how to stop it as words shove their way past my lips. "I'll be eighteen in two months."

Lakyn lifts an eyebrow, glancing over at me before he grins again and chuckles. "What makes you think I care how old you are?"

"Yeah, Daphne. You trying to climb on his dick since I wouldn't fuck you?" Aftyn chimes in from the backseat and I clench my jaw.

I can feel the blush in my cheeks, a burning heat that comes too easily with the curse of red hair and pale skin, and my tongue goes stiff and awkward again. I don't even know why I said it. I wasn't even thinking about it, or at least I don't *think* I was thinking about it. Still, the fact that he doesn't care that I'm not eighteen sends a thrill through my blood no matter what Aftyn says.

"You too busy fucking the blonde one?" Lakyn asks, glancing up at the rearview mirror and I bite back my smile.

"Willa was my best friend."

Taking a long drag on his cigarette, Lakyn blows the smoke out the window before running his tongue across his teeth, sucking on them. "And that means…?"

"No, we never fucked," Aftyn snaps and Lakyn lets out a laugh, tapping the heel of his hand on the steering wheel.

"Wait, so you're telling me you drove all the way out here with two chicks in the car, and you didn't get your dick wet even once?" Shaking his head, Lakyn laughs even louder before pointing at Aftyn in the rearview mirror. "I don't think you got much from me other than the looks, kid, and you obviously don't know what to do with that."

"Fuck you!"

"You sure you know how?" Lakyn keeps laughing and I turn to see Aftyn fuming in the backseat.

"I don't fuck guys. Guess that's something else I didn't inherit from you, *Pops*."

"Apparently you don't fuck much of anything, kid," Lakyn retorts, that wicked grin resting on his lips as his eyes return to the road in front of him for a moment before he looks at me. "Seems like you caught a break, Red. When it comes to members of the Scooby Gang, the kid clearly isn't able to deliver."

"I guess I did," I answer, unable to stop smiling as I listen to Aftyn huffing in the backseat. He's pissed off, but it's his own fault. Willa was never going to fuck him willingly, and he had too many feelings to take what he wanted from her. When I'd first got in the car with them, I'd been willing to take him for a test drive... but now? I think I'll set my sights a little higher.

Not that Lakyn has shown much interest yet, even when I took my shirt off, but maybe he's just waiting for me to prove myself. I ash the cigarette out the window and take another drag, reveling in the whirly feeling of the nicotine speeding its way through my bloodstream.

"How long is this bullshit road trip going to last? Because I'm not sure I can handle much more of this fan club shit without getting sick," Aftyn grumbles, flicking his cigarette out the window before he rolls it back up.

"Don't you know that life's supposed to be a journey?" Lakyn glances up at the rearview mirror. "Enjoy the ride. Take pleasure in the little things. All that bullshit that basically means shut up and don't start asking me 'are we there yet' or I'll cut your tongue out to save myself the trouble of *not* listening to you."

"You can try, *Pops*."

Tossing his cigarette, I love that Lakyn doesn't look the least bit concerned. It's his confidence, the absolute knowledge that he's in control of the world around him while Aftyn always seems to be fighting the universe. Wanting girls he can't have, seeking out family that didn't even know he existed, killing Willa's friend just so he didn't have to worry about the competition—it's pathetic. Clicking his tongue against the back of his teeth a few times, Lakyn finally looks up at the mirror again. "If you want to meet your auntie, kid, you might not want to test your luck before we're even out of town."

"Where the fuck is my aunt anyway?"

I watch as Lakyn tilts his head from side to side a few times before shrugging a shoulder. "She's wherever she thinks the devil wants her to be, but I know just the place to get an update on your errant Aunt Trixie."

"Yeah? And where's *that*? Or are you just making shit up as you go along?" Aftyn snaps, kicking at something in the floorboard.

"Try living in the moment, kid. Stop trying to figure everything out, because I'm definitely not going to tell you anything I haven't already decided I want you to know. Just sit back, shut up, and don't tempt me to make a decision about you before you've even tried to impress me."

"I don't give a shit if I impress you."

Lakyn chuckles, pushing a hand back through his hair before he gets comfortable in the seat, one hand draped over the top of the steering wheel. "Sure, kid."

They both fall silent, and I let my cigarette drop out the window before I roll it up and the lack of wind rushing past makes everything seem even quieter. It's hard to take my eyes off Lakyn, and I don't even know why I'm reacting like this. I've never felt anything like it, so I don't even have words for it, but I do know a few things.

One, Aftyn may not want to impress Lakyn, but I definitely do.

Two, he's dangerous and interesting and a killer like me.

And finally, I wasn't lying when I said '*I love Lakyn.*' I've never felt the emotion before, but I'm pretty sure this is it, and I'll do whatever it takes to stay on this side of the hatchet he carried over his shoulder like it was made for him.

I'll do whatever he wants.

## FIVE

## Blah, Blah, Blah

LAKYN

The Scooby girl keeps looking at me with stars in her eyes. The only redhead I can recall meeting before her that held my attention for a short time was Jizz Ball. Of course, *that* bitch turned out to be more trouble than she was worth.

She tried her hand at being the new and improved Beatrix St. Germain… and it worked for a while. Until I went and got the blonde who keeps ruining my life—even in her fucking absence—from where she was hiding at junkie central.

*Which reminds me.*

"Hey, kid?" I say, glancing into the rear-view. The boy who thinks he's hot shit because he got the best part of the family tree glares at me.

"My name is Aftyn."

"Great," I reply with a chuckle. "I've got a question for you."

He grunts as he looks down at some little strappy thing on his wrist then back at me. If that means something to him, and I'm sure it does, then I have more leverage on him. I shake my head as a smile starts to form on my lips. He gives up his weaknesses way too easily—I guess the Vegas bitch rubbed off on him.

"What was that exchange you had with Ichabod on the way out of my house?" I ask, my tone growing sterner. I don't mind fucking around and having a good time, but if he's been telling stories he shouldn't be, then I'll have to deal with that when I get back.

The kid shrugs as a shit-eating grin takes up half his face and I grit my teeth. *Is this how Ichabod and Trixie feel when I do that?*

"Cute," I say sarcastically. "But one thing you should know about me is that I do *not* like being lied to. So, whatever comes out of your mouth next had better be the fucking truth."

"I never lie," Red pipes up next to me. I glance at her for a moment and scoff. Her eyes are so wide and fucking adoring right now that it's all I can do not to push open the truck door and let her little ass tumble out onto the pavement.

"Ichabod? Oh, you mean your boyfriend, Pops? Well, how much time do you have? Actually, since no one seems to know where the fuck we're going, I'll give you the cliff notes version in case you decide we've gone far enough."

*Call him my boyfriend one more goddamn time, you little shit.*

"A few weeks ago, I started getting these weird emails. I was shopping online for Willa—I wanted to get her something nice because she's always been good to me. Not that you would know what it's like to be good to anyone from what I understand. Granted, that was Mom's version, but I will tell you that I paid for *all* of your fucking sins growing up. Anyway," he continues, as he sits up and leans on the back of Red's seat. "I decided to reply to the emails one day and the very next one I got a day or two later was a name, a few different addresses to try my hand at, and a dare."

I roll my eyes and reach for another cigarette. Clearly, he wasn't listening when I said I don't appreciate being lied to, or maybe he was and just doesn't give a fuck, but I'll listen to the rest of his horseshit and decide what to do when he's done.

"I finally managed to talk my best friend into this road trip thinking it would be the most amazing thing to happen to me. I figured, 'Hell, my father can't be worse than my mother,' and she agreed. I've never been more wrong in my entire life about an assumption, but that's not the point. The point is that when we left New York, the emails turned into text messages. Then I tried calling a few times and all I heard was heavy breathing, like some kind of fucking pervert. I'm sure he learned that from you though, right? To make a long story short…"

*Too late.*

"After this bitch killed the only person that's ever given a shit about me in my entire life—and I still owe you for that one," he says, smacking the back of Red's headrest. "You decided the best thing for us would be to get into my dead best friend's truck and head out to fuck-knows-where to meet some bitch that probably ditched your ass for a reason."

I suck my teeth.

"And where in all of that babbling did you tell me what the exchange between you and Ichabod was?" I ask in a bored tone.

"'Almost like looking into a mirror,'" he snarls at me.

"Huh?" I ask, turning slightly to steal a glance at him.

"That's what your fucking boyfriend said to me on the way out, and if you don't believe me, then here." He digs his phone out of his pocket and throws it in my lap missing my dick narrowly and I smirk. "Read it and weep, Pops. Looks like your guy there has his own secrets that you don't even know about."

Before I have a chance to tell him how full of shit I know he happens to be, Red's hand darts across the way and retrieves the kid's phone from where it landed between my legs. I roll my eyes at the interior roof when she uses the chance to let her fingers graze my dick. I'm no stranger to having chicks throw themselves at me, but she's being *too* desperate for it.

That's a no-go in my book.

I've never been a fan of nice and easy—I prefer to take what the fuck I want.

"Done copping your feel there, Daphne? Save some for his boyfriend. I'm sure he'll be sad to know that Pops stepped out on him again," the kid says cheerfully.

I lean over and backhand him in the face. He immediately looks shocked, then angry, and places a hand where I slapped him. Probably to ease the stinging sensation.

Not that I particularly give a shit.

I don't care about the fucking barbs he takes at Red, but he's gonna learn his place when it comes to me come hell or high water.

"Oops!" I say, mocking his cheerful tone. "Guess my hand slipped."

"I hate you!" he shouts at me as he throws himself back against the seat like a toddler having a temper tantrum. And if that's how he wants to behave, I'm not above belting him. But not right now. First, I have to set him straight.

"You know how I know you're a fucking liar?" I ask, grinning at him maliciously through the rearview. "Because Ichabod doesn't have a goddamn cell phone. There are no computers or fun little gadgets in my house that I don't have control over. Not to mention, he knows what happens if he tries to get a little brave. Now, before you start up with your bullshit again, there's a little something you need to know about me that your Mommy didn't tell you."

He pulls his legs up on the chair and keeps a hand on his face, refusing to look at me, but that's okay. He doesn't have to look—he only has to listen and understand.

"Anyone that ends up on my bad side usually doesn't get very far. Like I said before, your whore of a mother probably slipped away when I was asleep, but long drives take it out of me sometimes, so that's a mistake I can forgive myself for. What I didn't expect though, was for that fucking mistake to show up on my door and expect me to immediately embrace it and give a shit about it. There are only a few people I give a shit about, and you know who's at the top of that list? Not you. You're not even at the bottom of the fucking list, and if you keep lying to me about things, then you're more than likely going to end up at the top of another one of my favorite lists that you *don't* want to be on. Make no mistake about it, kid—son or not—I'll slit your fucking throat and leave you on the side of the road."

I glance over at Red, the grin spreading over my face when I see how in awe she suddenly is of me.

But now they know the rules.

Blood or no blood, cross me and I'll fucking take you down.

I turn my attention back toward the road in front of me and let out a heavy sigh before I reach for another smoke. *And speaking of being crossed; here we fucking go again.*

New Mexico. The Land of Enchantment.

I only ever cross state lines for one crazy bitch, and I'm not even sure how many years it's been since I graced her doorstep with my presence, but I'm sure she'll be excited.

"Come out, come out wherever you are," I mumble under my breath as I press down on the gas pedal toward the first stop on the road trip back to Hell.

## SIX

## Parking Lot Party Favors

AFTYN

I don't know what I expected from Lakyn Meyer, but a death threat in the first hour of meeting the asshole definitely hadn't hit my radar.

He thinks I was looking for some warm welcome, for him to hug me or whatever—and he's wrong. I never thought that would be the way this shit went. If anything, I thought whoever my sperm donor was would just deny being my father, I'd find out who was fucking with me and out them to the jackass, and then get back on the road with Willa.

*Willa.*

Just thinking her fucking name makes my chest hurt like someone punched me right in the center of it. Staring down at my lap, I tuck my thumb under her hair tie and roll it back and forth across my skin, watching the way it distorts my fingerprint. It's leaving a dark pressure ring behind, but my wrists are bigger than Willa's are... *were*.

Swallowing, I try not to think about how she used to take her hair down whenever we watched a movie, popping the little hair tie on her wrist so she wouldn't lose it. On those nights sometimes she'd lean against me, let me put an arm around her, and even if I copped a feel, she'd just smack my hand away with a laugh and we'd keep watching the movie.

Maybe things could have been different between us if I hadn't been so quick to back down, but she was the only other person I let in my universe. She helped me kill my whore of a mother, she helped set me free and then set me up with a place to live. She could be a raging bitch sometimes, and that bullshit with Dexter was annoying as fuck, but I still loved her.

She was my best friend... and now she's gone.

Because of me.

I snap the hair band on my wrist, letting the sting of pain soak into my flesh as I glare at the two fucks in the front seats. I may have dragged Willa into their line of fire, but Daphne actually did the deed, and Lakyn told her to do it.

Looking at the hatchet in the floorboard, I imagine what it would feel like to swing it, embedding it in Daphne's chest so that she'll choke on her blood like Wills did—except I won't slit her throat to end it faster. I'll let her suffocate on it, and I'll watch every last twitch of her body, so she knows exactly why she died. I don't think Lakyn would stop me if I went after Daphne, but I'll have to come up with something other than an outright attack to take him down. He's still got a few inches on me, and although I'm a hell of a lot younger than the asshole, he doesn't look out of shape.

*Patience.*

That's what I've got to do. Just be patient. Bide my fucking time until I can get revenge and add the matching patricide to my matricide. Mom would be so pissed to be joined in death by this asshole, and that's honestly just the cherry on top of this idea.

Cracking my neck to the side, I roll the window down and pop a cigarette between my teeth. Lighting it, I focus on the smoke moving in and out of my lungs instead of the irritating music my sperm donor has on the radio.

---

AN HOUR OR SO LATER, Lakyn suddenly swerves to change lanes, and I catch myself against the door of the car as he barely makes it onto the exit ramp. "What the fuck? Who taught you to drive?"

"Satan," Lakyn says over his shoulder, flashing a smirk at me in the mirror that pisses me off even more because it's the same damn smirk I sent his fucking boyfriend. I hate that we look so similar, it makes it impossible to deny that this motherfucker actually fucked *my* mother.

"Where are we going?" I ask and he rolls his eyes dramatically.

"We need some supplies if we're going to have a proper road trip," he answers as he pulls into a strip mall with a few larger stores and some smaller food places and other shit crammed in around them. I have no idea what supplies he's referring to, but I'm not really in the mood to harass him into talking to me anymore, so I leave it alone and just take another drag on my cigarette.

When Lakyn pulls into a parking spot, he leans forward, looking up through the windshield for a second, and then takes off again. He meanders around the parking lot a few times before finally parking in the very last row. Shoving the car into park, he turns around to lean on the center console, still wearing that fucking smirk. "Red and I are going to get some supplies, and you're going to pick us up a party favor for the road. I prefer blondes, but feel free to grab whoever you can."

"What?" I stare at him, confused, and he sighs, wiping a hand over his face.

"You"—he points at me, and then mimes his two fingers walking—"are going to walk around this place and find some chick to be our entertainment for the road. Where we're headed it's always a good idea to bring someone along that doesn't matter. Plus, I might get bored. Got it?"

"You want me to kidnap someone?" I don't quite believe that's what he's asking until his grin spreads and he claps his hands together sarcastically.

"Look at that, you figured it out, kid!" Lakyn turns back around and turns the car off, hopping out a second later to twist and stretch his back. I haven't moved though, and I'm not sure how the fuck he expects me to kidnap some chick in the middle of the fucking afternoon in a public place. Shit, I haven't *ever* kidnapped someone, but I'm pretty sure doing it in crowded, well-lit, public places is just about the dumbest way to go about it.

"I don't think he's kidding," Daphne says and I glare at her.

"Shut up."

She shrugs and opens her door, digging out a pair of sunglasses and a wallet before she shoves her backpack into the floorboard, but just as I think she's about to get out, she pauses and leans back to look at me again. "Just flirt with some girl and invite her to hang out with you. It's not complicated."

"Oh, so you've kidnapped people?" I ask before blowing a cloud of smoke right at her face.

Daphne's nose wrinkles and then she rolls her eyes. "I'm a girl, I don't *have* to kidnap anyone. People just come to me. Damsel in distress and all that shit."

"Right, cause you're so fucking hot that no one can look away."

A loud series of knocks at the window to my left makes me turn my glare on Lakyn through the glass as he messes with his hair in the reflection. Then he opens the door and leans on it, grinning at me like this is the best fucking idea he's ever had. "Going to puss out, kid?"

"No." I brush him aside to get out of the car and stomp my cigarette into the asphalt before holding out my hand. "Give me Willa's keys. I'm not getting left here so that you two can go fuck somewhere."

"Say please," Lakyn says, his voice taking on a quality that I'm sure he thinks is seductive—to guys that like dick anyway. When I don't say anything, or move my hand, he plucks the keys out of his pocket and holds them up, jingling them. "Well, now you have to say pretty please."

"Go to hell," I growl, walking away from him, and he starts laughing.

"That's exactly where we're headed, kid, but you've gotta get the party favor." Lakyn is tossing the keys in the air and catching them now, over and over. I grind my teeth as I try to decide if it's worth the risk leaving Wills' car keys with him.

*No. Definitely not.*

"I'll go get a goddamn blonde *party favor* if you give me the fucking keys."

Lakyn leans forward slightly, cupping his hand beside his ear, and I imagine jabbing Daphne's knife right through his ear and into his brain. It's a nice little fantasy that lets me calm down enough to remember that I'm trying to play the long game with this asshole until I get the chance to end him myself.

"Please," I bite out through clenched teeth and he laughs.

"So fucking close, kid. But you need to listen when I speak or you're going to find yourself roadside sooner rather than later." He jingles the keys again and I force myself to act like I don't give a shit.

Painting a smirk on my face, I shove my hand back through my hair and glance up at the blue sky, making *him* wait for a minute before I finally look at him again. "Sure, Pops. *Pretty* please can I have the fucking keys?"

Lakyn doesn't even respond, he just tosses them at my chest, and I manage to catch them, tightening my fist so that the sharp edges dig into my palm as he walks past me toward the cunt that's first on my list to die. Daphne smiles at him, and I'm not sure why I ever thought she was attractive, or innocent. Now that I've been around her, I can see the frayed edges of crazy in her eyes—but neither of them are my problem right now.

"Half an hour, kid!" Lakyn shouts over his shoulder as the two of them head toward one of the big box stores, and I groan as I slam the door of the truck and lock it.

I take out my phone to check the time, and then scan the line of stores and restaurants and shit. All of them probably have cameras, and when I glance up at the light poles, I can see bubbles for cameras closer to the storefronts. It's why Lakyn parked all the fucking way out here. Shaking my head, I pop the back of the SUV and dig through my bag for a baseball cap and my sunglasses. If Lakyn's plan is to screw me over by getting my face plastered all over the goddamn news, he's going to have to do better than that.

He'll have to bury that fucking hatchet in my back himself.

*Shit, the hatchet.*

I move it into the back of the SUV, lock it up, and then pull the brim of the cap low and head toward the smaller shops and restaurants.

---

TWENTY MINUTES.

It's taken me twenty fucking minutes to find this blonde bitch, and she's already salivating over my attention. I can't tell how old she is, probably early twenties, but I'd probably have a better idea if I was even remotely paying attention to whatever the fuck she's been talking about for the last five minutes—which is already more time than I really have to spare.

"So..." I cut her off, keeping my back to the only camera in this shitty little shop as I turn on my most charming smile, the one that's never failed to get a girl into bed when I wanted it. As much as I hate it, Daphne's bullshit suggestion is just about the only way I can pull this off in the time Lakyn gave me. "I was about to leave, but I don't really want to end this. Would you wanna hang out for a bit?"

"Where are you going?" she asks, smiling at me as she tugs on her shirt, lowering her neckline just a little, and I let my eyes go where she obviously wants them before I bring them back to hers with a chuckle.

"Well, I had planned on grabbing some stuff, but if you just want to go somewhere and get to know each other better"—I shrug—"I'm down for that."

"Um, wow..." She giggles, blushing as she glances down at her phone and then out the windows before she looks at me again, tracing her tongue across her bottom lip in what I'm sure she thinks is a sexy face, but it looks more like she's trying to find crumbs from whatever shit she ate for lunch. "Do you live near here?"

"Yeah," I lie easily, it's never been hard for me, and I can tell she's so close to giving in, so I tug on the line to reel her in. Pushing a hand back through my hair, I take a step toward the door. "But if you're not interested, that's cool. I can just—"

"Wait." She wavers, and then she seems to make a decision and closes the gap between us, her hand reaching for mine, and I let her interlace our fingers as I flash a grin at her and lead the way out the door.

Once we're in the parking lot, I let go of her hand and toss an arm around her shoulder. Then I pull her closer and lean down to whisper in her ear, "Somehow you look even better in the sunlight."

"Yeah?" she giggles again, and I wish I'd paid attention to her name, but since the first three bitches I talked to didn't pan out, I hadn't expected this one to actually agree. I'd already had my eye on another blonde that I'd seen walk into one of those tacky girl stores filled with cheap jewelry and make-up and hair shit—but this one is already halfway to the truck and slipping her arm around my waist as she fishes for compliments. "You really think so?"

*In the bag with time to spare, now I just have to keep her entertained.*

"Yeah." I nod, scanning the area around the SUV for any sign of Lakyn or Daphne, but I don't see them yet. "You caught my eye in that place and I just knew I had to talk to you. Guess it's my lucky day, right?"

"Guess so." She lifts her chin, a little self-satisfied smile curving her lips, and it makes me want to shove her face down on the asphalt. If I didn't need to her to believe she was the hottest piece of ass I've ever seen right now, I'd be more than happy to take her narcissistic ass down a few pegs—but if Lakyn's bullshit is real then I'll get to do more than that to this chick before the day is over.

When we get to the truck, she tries to peel off for the passenger door, but I tug her to the far side of the car and gently press her back against the door. Taking off my hat, I toss it on the roof before pushing my sunglasses to the top of my head. I lean back to look her over, grinning.

"Sorry, there's just something about you…" I let my voice trail off as I bring my gaze to her lips and she laughs a little, her smile widening. Her hands land on my waist to pull me closer, and I return the favor.

"Your eyes are unreal," she whispers, but I have to fight the urge to roll them. Sure, I used to like how girls reacted to my blue eyes, but now that I've met the asshole they came from—the charm has sort of worn off.

"Thanks, I think I'm a little more focused on your lips right now. They make me want to…" Closing the gap, I lean down and kiss her. Softly at first, but with the first little sound she makes, I crank it up. I nip her lip before delving in, pressing her harder against the side of the SUV, and the whore moans like she's auditioning for a goddamn porno. Fortunately, no one else felt like parking at the back of the fucking lot.

"We should go to your place," she pants as she turns out of the kiss, all breathy and irritating because she's fucking *talking* but I just trail my lips down her throat, pretending to be too caught up in touching her to respond.

I'm not even picturing this bitch anymore—I'm thinking about Willa. I'm thinking about the way her shampoo smelled, and how whenever she dropped her goddamn guard for a minute, she would melt against me just like this. The cunt ruins my train of thought by pushing at my chest, and it takes more self-restraint than I expect to stop myself from pinning her wrists against the windows.

"Come on, Carter, let's go." There's an edge of a whine to her voice, and for a second I'm more than just irritated because I forgot I'd given her a bullshit name. Leaning away from her, I glance toward the back of the SUV and shake my head a bit when I realize they're still not back yet.

*Thirty fucking minutes. Bullshit.*

"Just a few more minutes," I say, moving in to continue kissing her, but she pushes at my chest again and this time I grab her wrist.

"Ow!" she shouts, yanking her arm free before she shoves me harder. "What is this, Carter? Are you waiting for friends or something?"

"No, I—"

"Then what the fuck were you looking at?" Moving past me, she walks to the end of Willa's SUV and then turns to stare at me. "Is this some fucking prank? You get some girl to make out with you in a parking lot and your friends record it and post it?"

"That's not it." I grab her arm as she tries to walk away again, but she starts screaming like a fucking psycho.

"Let go of me! I'm not going anywhere with you! HELP! SOMEONE!"

I let her go as soon as she really gets loud, raising my hands to my shoulders. "Chill out, okay? I thought we were having fun."

"Yeah, fuck off, douchebag. You're not that hot, and I'm not that stupid." She flips me off as she moves backward. "Go jack off while thinking about me, loser."

I'm so damn tempted to just grab her and shove her in the back of the truck, but it's broad daylight and I still don't see Lakyn or Daphne, which means I'd have to knock her out, and it's way too likely someone would see us struggling. So, I let her walk away and then I slam my fist into the door, cursing under my breath when pain radiates across my knuckles—but it's not a bad thing.

Pain at least reminds me I'm still alive.

---

IT'S BEEN ALMOST fifty minutes since we separated when I finally hear voices and then someone smacking their hand against the back window. Muttering under my breath, I reach over to the keys and push the button to pop the rear open. I hear Lakyn laugh, and I glance back in time to see him leave Daphne to unload the bags while he walks to the driver door.

Lakyn swings it open with a manic grin, leaning on the roof as he looks around the inside of the SUV dramatically. "Something's missing, kid."

I lean against the window and cross my arms, offering a casual shrug. "If you'd come back to the car on time, you'd have your fucking blonde party favor, but she wouldn't wait."

"What part of *get a fucking party favor* was complicated to you?" he asks, head tilting to the side, and I roll my eyes.

"We're in public, and it's the middle of the goddamn afternoon. What was I supposed to do, knock her out? Dig the knife out of the cunt's backpack and threaten her to sit quietly in the car until you decided to show up?" I grab my pack of smokes off the dash and light up, rolling my window down to let the smoke drift out of my mouth slowly. When I glance back to Lakyn, I realize he hasn't moved, but the smile on his face looks a lot more feral as he sucks his teeth, running his tongue over them.

"Look, kid... If you're expecting me to hold your hand through this shit, you might as well give that up right now. You'll either step up or I'll bury my hatchet in your fucking skull and forget about you by morning." Lakyn stands up straight, looking back at Daphne before he stares at me again. "Me and Red got the party supplies, *you* were supposed to get the party favor. I don't really give a shit how you were going to do it as long as you held up your end."

"Yeah, well, she's gone," I answer, grinning at him. "Next time, don't be late."

The rear of the SUV slams shut, and Daphne pauses by my window before she opens the back. "We switching seats?"

"Shut up and get in." Lakyn doesn't even look at her as he climbs behind the wheel and shuts the door hard enough to rock the car.

"No party favor?" Daphne asks, and I take another drag off my cigarette instead of answering her.

Lakyn shakes his head, laughing quietly as he turns the car toward the exit. "No. Seems like the kid is more of a fuck-up than I thought. He lost the party favor, which means I'll have to show him how it's done."

"At least we have the rope and duct tape now, and all the other stuff." Her voice is so goddamn *happy* about the fucking 'party supplies' that Lakyn grabbed, and I don't bother pointing out that if I'd had that shit, I could have dealt with the blonde. Daphne leans forward, obviously trying to see Lakyn better. "Do you want me to get someone?"

"Fucking Christ. No more talking or I'll slit your throat too and just head back home." Lakyn doesn't even glance at her as he taps the radio on and turns it up. More old music for the old man.

I don't have a fucking clue how old he is, but however many years he's survived on this planet, his fucking days are numbered.

## SEVEN

## Home is For the Hopeless

ICHABOD

Something useful that I learned from Lakyn is how to clean up after he makes messes. For a while, after I moved in with him, it was all I did.

Well, that and be his favorite thing to brutalize, but I worked my way up rather quickly. I think agreeing with him that he helped me get straight served his ego rather nicely.

After almost twenty years of being his stepping stool, he's actually been a little nicer to me.

And if Aftyn doesn't tell him what I've been up to behind his back, then it'll probably stay that way.

Not that I trust him.

Or Lakyn.

Hell, I don't even trust myself anymore most days because I never thought I would do something like this.

Manipulation has always been in Bea's bag of tricks, but not mine.

A genuine smile—something I haven't felt in years—appears on my lips. Just the thought of seeing Bea again after so long has me feeling so much better.

I know that Lakyn will bring her back since he promised to, and the thing about him is that he never breaks a pact once he seals it.

I wonder if she'll look the same. I don't think age will have done a goddamn thing to Bea, and if it tried, she probably gutted it and watched it gurgle.

I begin to whistle as I drag the garbage bag full of the girl—uh, Willa I think her name was—toward the back of the house. I feel bad that she became a casualty in Lakyn's little war, but she's blonde. And while manipulating people may be Bea's thing, annihilating blondes—or having someone else do it so he can mentally get off—is Lakyn's.

*I should have told Aftyn to come alone,* I think as the smile falters on my lips. I always feel bad when someone dies because of Lakyn, but… I don't know. I guess I feel worse since I've survived this long and, to my knowledge, no one else has.

Bumping the door with my back a few times gets it to open as I drag the bag inside.

Well, that's not entirely true. At least a few others have survived—there was the entire Vegas debacle. God knows where that big guy is these days, though I imagine that if Lakyn ever bumped into him again, it would more than likely end with one of them dead.

*Hm.*

I groan as I roll my eyes and let the bag go.

I feel bad for even thinking it would be okay to try to find the man and tell him to show up.

Lakyn may be older, but he hasn't slowed down in the least, and that means the only one who would die would be the surprise guest.

*Kind of like you,* I think as I open the bag and start to pull out body parts.

Once I've got all of the bits and pieces resting on the bag, I head over to the large, rusty tub that Lakyn keeps in the corner of the room.

Just above it is an array of hatchets. All of them are handcrafted by the devil that takes the greatest delight in using them.

His favorite he never leaves in this room, though.

Always seeing the single empty rung makes me liken him to Dorian Gray.

Almost as if he spent too much time looking at the hatchet, then it might show him who he really was.

Of course, considering it's Lakyn, he'd probably get off on that too.

Running a hand back through my hair, I step over what's left of Willa and walk over to the large cabinet where Lakyn likes to keep more of his toys. Once I locate a few gallon bottles of acid, I grab one and make a couple of trips back and forth until I have the three that he expressly told me I would need the first time I did this.

Carefully, I unscrew the cap and begin to fill the tub. When it's half full, I place the second bottle down and go back toward the bag. I pull it over to the tub and start placing the body parts inside.

As soon as the poor girl is submerged, I empty the second bottle, then the third, before I go sit on Lakyn's workbench and begin to pick thoughtfully at my fingernails.

Everything will get better when I see Bea again and I can't wait.

## EIGHT

## Running with Scissors

DAPHNE

I can't get over the fact that Aftyn has disappointed Lakyn. I can feel the tension from the front of the truck, but it's more from his side than his dad's.

*God, I love him,* I think wistfully as Lakyn clears his throat and continues to tap his fingers on the steering wheel.

"Can you just let me out?" Aftyn suddenly asks. "I don't want to be in this fucking truck anymore. Not without Willa."

"Don't make my hand slip again, kid," Lakyn replies cheerfully as he continues drumming his fingers to the beat of the song.

"Want me to kill him?" I ask from the backseat. Aftyn turns to glare at me over his shoulder and Lakyn lets out a laugh.

I made him laugh again and that's all that matters to me, but if he wants more blood, I'd be willing to claim it.

"No thanks, Red," Lakyn replies as he glances at me in the rearview mirror. "I want him to meet his Aunt Beatrix. Maybe after."

He smirks at Aftyn who's turned to face him. I can see how angry he is because his neck is crimson, but instead of speaking back, Aftyn shifts to face the windshield and slumps in the seat.

I think it's nice that he's finally listening to his father. After all, isn't that what good children are supposed to do?

I've never been a good kid, and I don't even remember my parents, but if Lakyn was my daddy I'd probably be inclined to listen. They go quiet and I lean back in the seat, laying the side of my head against the cool glass. It still smells like that bitch in here, so I'll have to do something about that eventually.

I never did have a car of my own, but I think Lakyn would let me have this one considering he probably won't want it after we get back.

But I decide not to let my thoughts settle on Willa. Not when I can still smell the faint scent of dried blood just underneath where my chin is.

Based on what I saw, it doesn't seem realistic that those two had the balls to off anyone themselves. Even though Aftyn told Willa he killed Dexter... no one actually saw the body. Although, by now I'm pretty confident that when Aftyn said this was supposed to be a two-person trip, he meant it.

He could have just knocked the other guy out though and left him in the bathroom.

"Hey," I say, reaching around and tapping him on his shoulder.

Aftyn jumps damn near out of his skin as he swats my hand away and glares at my reflection in the side mirror.

"Don't fucking touch me," he barks.

Lakyn chuckles but doesn't intercede. I think he's interested by the possible exchange we're going to have, so I may as well make it worth his while.

"You never did tell me about this bloodstain," I say as innocently as I can. "Did Willa do it? It must have been her 'cause it doesn't seem like you've got the best parts of your dad inside of you. You just wear it where it can be seen like a mask, but you suppress the rest. How come?"

Lakyn lets out an impressed, low whistle.

I grin and decide to dig at Aftyn a little deeper when he just grits his teeth harder.

"Or maybe you just got your period? Is that what happened? I think that'd be more believable than you taking out Willa's bestie." I glance over at his dad. "Hey, Lakyn? Maybe we should stop for tampons at some point. Don't know if Aftyn's pussy has dried up yet."

Suddenly my head jerks back and light explodes in front of my eyes. A searing pain begins to burn through my face as I hit the back seat and immediately raise my hands to my face.

"I told you to shut the fuck up," Aftyn seethes quietly.

I blink rapidly a few times trying to shake the cobwebs away and my eyes water when the pain starts to take hold. I'm not crying because he hurt my feelings, hell, it's the most impressive thing he's done so far. It's just the body's natural reaction to being sucker punched by a crybaby.

"Didn't think you had it in you," Lakyn tells him with a smirk. "But try not to do that again, eh?"

"You want some too?" Aftyn snaps at him.

Lakyn laughs good-naturedly as he goes back to his music and to ignoring his son.

Though I'm honestly starting to doubt the parentage here. Aftyn may look like Lakyn, yet he doesn't seem to have his confidence. Or at the very least, he lost it back in the woods somewhere—if he had any part in killing that couple at all.

I reach for my backpack and start rifling around inside of it. The knife I took from the woods still has flecks of Willa's blood near the handle and, apparently, Aftyn wants to join her.

Which is quite fine by me, and probably Lakyn too.

I pull the knife out and start to move toward Aftyn when the truck suddenly swerves onto the side of the road.

I hit the door hard because I wasn't expecting it, and I almost end up cutting myself too.

"What the fuck?" Aftyn barks at Lakyn, who's watching me through the rearview mirror.

"Get out, kid. I think we need some rules," he tells Aftyn, his eyes still on me. "You wait here, Red. This won't take long at all."

Aftyn lets out a loud sigh as he pushes his door open. Lakyn cuts the engine to the truck and slips the keys into his pocket before he climbs out the driver's side.

I lean forward, propping my forearm against the back of Aftyn's seat, knife still in my other hand as I watch the scene unfold in front of the truck.

Aftyn looks like he's ready for a fight and Lakyn looks like he's amused by how puffed up he is. He leans against the hood of the truck and pulls out his pack of cigarettes, offers one to his son, then lights them both.

Curiosity starts to shoot through me, but it feels different this time. Almost like when your foot falls asleep and no matter how many times you slap it, you can't wake it up.

Lakyn scratches the back of his head before he finally begins to talk. I wish I could hear what they're saying, but since he took the keys I can't open the damn back window to listen in.

It's just mutters.

Angry.

Quiet.

Amused.

Secret.

Lakyn nods in the direction of the windshield at one point and I watch as Aftyn crosses his arms tightly over his chest before he runs a hand irritably over his face, then nods.

In agreement? Defeat?

I don't fucking know because I can't hear.

A few more moments pass as they both stand outside in abject silence, Lakyn with his back toward the truck as he leans on the hood, and Aftyn glancing up and down the road.

When they both finally toss their cigarettes, I sit back like the obedient little girl I can be—and wait.

But once they're back inside the truck, in their respective seats, I arch an eyebrow curiously as they both turn and glance at me for a moment.

Lakyn with that damn half-grin on his face.

Aftyn with malice and danger in his eyes.

Something is up, but if they think I'm just going to sit around and take whatever the fuck it is, I'll show them what I'm really made of.

"Ready?" Lakyn asks as he turns around and fishes the keys out of his pocket.

"Ready as I'll ever be!" I reply cheerfully.

He sucks his teeth as he turns the truck back on and then pulls onto the road.

I'll show him that I deserve to be a part of his family, and if there's only room for one, I'll prove that he needs me more than he'll ever need Aftyn. Then we can be happy together.

And if there's only one spot in Lakyn's family at all… then I'll just have to get rid of that guy at his house when we get back too.

Because I know there's no one else on this fucking planet that will ever accept me like Lakyn Meyer would, and I'll do whatever it takes to earn that from him. To not lose this chance where I'll never have to hide again. I'll never have to hitchhike again.

*Where I'll finally have an actual home.*

## NINE

## Origins of Evil

LAKYN

It's been twenty years since I passed the city limits of Albuquerque and the memories bring a grin to my lips. Fucking Trixie and her Satanic church. All the chaos we caused when she was still on her mission to be Lucifer's number one bitch.

Those were good times.

As I monitor the exits, trying to remember which one led to the birthplace of Beatrix's crazy, I suddenly remember Trixie riding Basil on the floor of her fucking house with my cock in her mouth. I groan under my breath, reaching down to adjust my dick behind my zipper. Fuck, that psycho princess could suck a golf ball through a garden hose... but she'd never spread those damn legs for me. Maybe this time she'll let me bend her over for old times' sake.

Angling toward the old neighborhood, I'm surprised by how easily I find her house again. There's a bunch of fucking plants outside now, and weird little garden gnomes, and I toss the truck into park and hop out without saying a word to either of the kids in the car. This isn't an official stop, but sometimes I've just got to satisfy my curiosity. I rap my knuckles on the door, running a hand back through my hair as I turn on my charming smile.

"Um, hello." The old guy that opens the door looks confused as hell, but I'm not surprised. There's no reason why I'd be on his doorstep if it wasn't making me think of the first time Ichabod opened it. If I'd brought *him* along, he'd probably appreciate this moment a little more than the idiot gaping at me right now.

"What the hell are we doing here?" the kid shouts from the SUV, and I roll my eyes, looking at the old guy.

"Kids, what are you gonna do?" I say, chuckling as I lean against the door frame, sneaking a peek at the living room that looks nothing like it did when Trixie lived here. The fat asshole in front of me closes the door part of the way, narrowing his eyes on me. "A friend of mine used to live here, I was just curious if I could take a look around."

"No, I don't think so." He shakes his head, pushing the door a little further closed, but I drop my foot against it to stop him.

"Come on. Just a quick peek." I flash another smile at him, just as a woman's voice echoes from deeper inside the house calling him 'Eddie.' Tilting my head, I look over his head as the bitch I assume is his wife appears in the living room. "Eddie... I just want to take a look around. Five minutes, tops."

"Who's this?" she asks, and I'm getting irritated by all the fucking stalling when all I want to do is walk around inside for a few minutes.

"Are we stopping for party favors?" Daphne shouts from beside the SUV and I clench my jaw as I turn to look at the two of them, waving them back into the damn truck.

"Oh, are those your kids?" the woman asks, nudging her husband aside as she smiles at me, and I chuckle because it doesn't seem to matter how old a chick is, they all want me.

"Basically," I answer with a shrug, but then she eases the door further closed until it bounces against my shoe. "I was just telling Eddie here that my friend used to live here, and I was wondering if I could just take a look around for a minute. Memories and all that."

"Well, it's getting late and we were about to have dinner. Maybe another—"

"That sounds great! We haven't had anything to eat all afternoon." Leaning my shoulder into the door, I push it open easily. The two of them way too weak to hold the door against me, and I whistle at the two idiots in the car. "Come on, kids! Dinner is served!"

"You can't just come in!" Eddie shouts and I wink at him as I stroll into the living room. They've got weird taste, and I don't really get what the fuck they're trying to go for other than… old people house. A bunch of knick-knack shit on the tables and shelves, and not a single piece of furniture seems to match.

"Please, we don't have anything you'd want to steal," Eddie's wife says, and I look her over from head to toe.

"Obviously."

"Thank you so much, we really are hungry," Red says from behind me, and I laugh as she pulls the sweet little girl act out of left field. Eddie doesn't seem to know what to do about her, and that gives the kid plenty of time to walk in behind her.

"Well, I—"

"So, what's for dinner?" I ask, tilting my head for a moment before I snap my fingers. "You know, I don't think Eddie mentioned your name."

"Gladys," she answers, smiling on reflex, before she shakes it off. "But, like I was trying to say, we really don't have enough food for all of you."

"Oh, don't worry about them. They're not that hungry anyway. Are you, kids?" I ask, glancing back at them where Red shakes her head and the kid just folds his arms and glares at me from beside the door. "See? No need to feed them."

"You need to leave. Right now," Eddie says, walking up behind me, and he's so much shorter than me that it's hard to resist the temptation to pat him on the head, instead I just throw an arm around his shoulders and drag him along as I wander back toward Trixie's old kitchen.

"I definitely have some shit to do tonight, but I just wanted to see the old place, you know?" I squeeze his flabby bicep as I wave a hand across the kitchen, remembering exactly where Basil's body was on the other side of the island. Letting Eddie go, I clap my hands together, rubbing them as I walk around to stare down at it. "Man, this place was in a lot better shape last time I was here. You guys just lazy, or too old for that home improvement shit?"

"Excuse me!" Gladys says, and I laugh, popping myself up onto the island as I look over the pots on the stove.

"Food doesn't exactly smell that great either," I add, grinning when Eddie starts wagging a finger at me.

"You're gonna leave right now, or I'm going to— AHH!" He starts screaming when I bend his finger sideways, but it's probably because the bone snapped like a twig. Still, he's fucking loud, so I plant my shoe in his chest and shove him away to shut him up, watching as he bounces off the stove, spilling one of the pots before he lands on the floor, shouting some more as the hot liquid of whatever was in it drips onto him. Hopping down, I kick him in the face, and I'm pretty sure I hear another crack amidst all the noise.

"Huh, apparently osteoporosis is a real issue." Grinning, I tilt my head toward Red and the kid, and they manage to catch Gladys before she has the chance to run off. Between the two of them, they force her back into the kitchen, and I'm not surprised that Red looks like it's Christmas fucking morning, while Aftyn looks bored as fuck. Gladys is babbling about not hurting them, which doesn't bother me, but when she starts screaming for help, I rub my forehead. "Kid, you obviously don't have an issue hitting women. Handle that, will you?"

The dull smack of flesh doesn't sound interesting enough for me to watch, and instead I peruse the various pots on the stove, picking up a spoon to taste what's left of the soup that Eddie is currently bathing in at my feet. It's bland and full of vegetables and I sigh, disappointed.

"This really isn't a great meal, Gladys. I'm sure Eddie would agree with me if he wasn't chewing on his teeth right now." I glance down when I feel a hand on my ankle and yank it out of Eddie's grip, bringing my heel down on his face again and again until he stops reaching for me. "That's just rude, Eddie. Don't you know you're not supposed to touch people without asking?"

"Pl-please don't hurt me," Gladys blubbers, and the kid rolls his eyes next to her.

"Don't get ahead of yourself," I say, grinning as I hop back onto the island to look at her. She's got a red spot on her cheek near her eye, and I'm guessing that's where the kid popped her.

*Good for him, maybe his balls are finally dropping.*

"Really, all I wanted to do was swing by my friend's old house and take a walk around, but Eddie there was just so fucking rude. Shit, it was *my* friend that used to live here. Technically that means she's got more of a right to say who's welcome here or not."

"We've lived here for fifteen years!" the old bitch argues, and I groan, waving a hand at the kid and he catches her around the throat this time, squeezing to keep her quiet, which I guess works fine.

"Well, I got my invitation over twenty years ago, so... first come, first served and all that." I shrug and look over the two of them. Eddie doesn't look so good on the floor, and I'm not completely sure if he's breathing anymore—not that it matters. They made their decisions when they wouldn't let me in Trixie's house for a simple look around.

"What the fuck are we doing here?" the kid asks, not paying attention to the old chick's weak tugging at his hand.

"Your Aunt Beatrix used to live here, and I just wanted to stop by, check it out." I lean to the side, tilting my head toward the floor. "She fucked this guy named Basil on the floor over here. He was already dead at that point, but it wasn't a big deal. She needed his dick for Lucifer's toy box or something like that. Honestly, I've never been great at paying attention to all the crazy shit Trixie says."

"So... are we done?"

"Not quite, kid." I chuckle and tug the cigarettes out of my jacket, popping one between my teeth before I pat my pockets and realize the damn lighter is in the car. "Shit." Hopping down again, I shove the shitty pot of soup out of the way and use the burner on the stove to light it, taking a long inhale of smoke before I let it out.

"What do you want us to do?" Red asks, and I grin at her. If she talked less, I think she'd actually have a chance at being useful for longer than I'm currently thinking of letting her breathe... but for now I might as well take advantage of having my own personal cult member.

"We're going to visit some of Aunt Beatrix's old friends in a little bit, and it's always nice to bring a gift along when stopping by unannounced." I shrug, taking another drag. "Or, that's what I've heard anyway."

Daphne is looking at me with those wide gray-brown eyes, and I decide now is as good a time as any to test her faith a bit.

"Why don't you put your heart into choosing something extra special to bring?" I say, and she looks over at Gladys with a smile that confirms just how ill-acquainted reality and Red are. "Just don't get too messy, okay? We've got somewhere to be."

---

FORTY-FIVE MINUTES later the kid is sitting in what I'm guessing used to be Eddie's chair, holding the Tupperware with our surprise in his lap. He didn't throw up, or pussy out, and even though he got annoyed that Daphne stripped down to her underwear to cut Gladys open, he still watched her play with the knives in the kitchen.

Crazy little bitch had blood everywhere, so I sent her off to the shower after she packed up the present. The garage had a few handy things, including two containers of gasoline for a lawn mower, and a couple of propane tanks. I've got one propane tank on top of each of the rude fucks who wouldn't give me five minutes to wander around Trixie's old house or offer us a bit of their shitty dinner.

The lack of neighborly behavior is pretty disappointing the more I think about it, and as I continue pouring gasoline around the living room, I jerk my chin at the kid to make him move. He huffs and stomps toward the door, leaving me chuckling in the living room as I splash some on the curtains before trailing it down the hallway, abandoning the first container in a bedroom to go grab the other one and continue my final tour of the house.

It's really kind of fitting to leave this place in ashes. When Trixie and Ichabod left, the house lost its soul, and that just isn't good for a place where so many memories existed. Hell, I'm doing this fucking neighborhood a favor. Gladys and Eddie were probably shitty people to live next to anyway.

"Hurry it up, Red!" I shout down the hall, and she pops out of the bathroom like she was just waiting for me to summon her.

"I'm ready," she says, and I have to admit she did a good job. Not a speck of blood on her anywhere.

Shoving the gas can into her hands, I point to the back of the house. "Finish emptying that out, I'm going to get the fireworks ready to go."

The kid gives me a look when I walk past him, but I just suck my teeth and head back into the kitchen. Turning all the burners on high, I grab a few of the dish towels and toss them on top before I turn around and give a whistle, marching back to the front door.

"Time to go," I call out, and Red comes back down the hall, throwing the empty gas can into the living room as she meets us at the door. When I glance outside, I notice that Aftyn has already lit a cigarette on the front walk and I hold my hand out. "Give me that, kid."

"I just lit it," he complains, and I snap my fingers and hold my hand out again. After an exaggerated eye roll, he huffs and walks the cigarette over to me. "Of course, Pops. Here you go."

Grinning, I tilt my head toward the truck. "Go on, get in."

I wait for them to climb in the SUV before I give one last look at Trixie's place as I take a long drag to get the end nice and hot before I flick it toward the living room and slam the door shut. Using my jacket, I wipe off the doorknob, and then saunter back to the car.

When I crank the SUV on and pull away, I catch the subtle flicker of flames through the living room window, and I can't help but think how fitting it is that my last view of her place looks like hell took up residence inside.

Sometimes things just work out the way they're supposed to.

By the time I swing the car by Ichabod's old place, the sun is already setting, and I know we don't have time for another walk down memory lane. Not that I ever spent any time there, but I could have brought him back a little souvenir or something to help him remember how good I've been for him, keeping him off the drugs and shit. Still, it's more important to find out where the hell the psycho princess has run off to, and there's only one place to go for that info since she cleared out of Ichabod's old drug den years ago.

It doesn't take long before I'm pulling into the Light of Lucifer parking lot, and more memories spin around in my head as I grab a space. When I glance at the rearview mirror, I can almost see Trixie in Red's psycho face, but when I look at the passenger seat absolutely nothing about the kid reminds me of Ichabod.

Ich has always worshiped me. He wanted my dick the first moment I showed up on Trixie's doorstep, and he's damn lucky that I'm still giving it to him after all these years—but this fucking kid doesn't show me the respect I'm due.

Still, I told the idiot he'd get to meet his Aunt Beatrix, and I tend to keep my promises.

"Wait… this is that Satanic church," the kid mumbles, leaning forward as the last rays of the sun turn the sky to a red haze above it. Honestly, it's the kind of dramatic fucking entrance that I deserve coming back to this place, and with all the cars in the parking lot this evening… I know my visit is going to be a welcome one.

"Sure is," I answer, sucking on my teeth as I turn the car off and shift in my seat to look at them both. Aftyn is frowning, Daphne has that wide-eyed shit that is starting to rub me the wrong way, and neither of them are likely to be much help inside with getting information—but I've always been a giver. "Your Aunt Beatrix used to be the number one bitch here. Head Priestess, or whatever they fucking called it, but if anyone has an idea where she's moved on to… it'll be these little wannabes."

"They worship Satan?" Red asks, and I click my tongue against my teeth as I turn to stare at her, waiting for her to sink back in her seat before I face forward again. She's been a decent little follower today, but that doesn't mean I'm in the mood to play twenty stupid questions with her.

"Anyway… we're going to go in and say hi. I'll grace their sanctum with my presence again, and we'll see what info they'll share. Then we'll go and find your auntie." Reaching behind the passenger seat, I drag my fingers over the floorboard, searching for my hatchet, but I can't reach it. Leaning between the seats, I angle myself back and realize the damn thing is gone. "Okay. Where the fuck is my hatchet?"

"What?" Daphne says, but I'm looking at Aftyn. He's got that goddamn smirk on his face, his arms crossed.

"Well, kid?" I prompt, and he glances over at me.

"Missing something?" he asks and I slam my forearm into his throat hard, wiping that fucking smirk off his face as he chokes, wheezing in air through an injured windpipe, and I let my grin spread as his face turns redder than the crazy bitch's hair in the backseat.

I light up a cigarette while he sputters, cracking the door to let it drift outside where a few random denizens of the night are moving toward the entrance to the church. Cracking my neck, I wait for him to manage a few halfway decent breaths before I continue. "Last chance, where's my hatchet, kid?"

He jerks a thumb at the back of the SUV and I barely have to glance at Daphne before she unbuckles her seat belt and bends over the backseat to dig around in the trunk space. Tilting my head at her wiggling ass, I decide that fucking her isn't completely off the table.

Maybe the kid just needs some help figuring out how it all works. Needs a little fatherly advice—insert dick into useless cunt, repeat until done. Dispose as needed.

"Found it!" Red calls out cheerily, lifting it up with a manic smile before she sits back down and I rip it from her fingers, checking it over to make sure the fucker didn't mess it up. I've got other toys at home, but there's something special about this one. It always just *feels* the best. Plus, on this trip it has some real goddamn meaning.

Once I'm satisfied that he didn't damage it, I reach over and bring the blunt side of it under the kid's chin, lifting his head up. "You know how we were talking about rules before? Here's another one. Touch my fucking hatchet again, and I'll bury it in your spine. Got it?"

Aftyn clears his throat, barely nodding his chin. "Yeah."

"Great!" I swing the hatchet over my shoulder, grinning again. "Let's go meet the children of the night."

Grabbing the keys, I hop out of the truck and tuck them into my pocket, stretching out my back as I grin at a blonde bitch dressed all in black who is eye-fucking me from the walkway. She smiles back, and I chuckle to myself as the two kids finally get out.

*Sometimes shit is just too easy for me.*

"Don't forget our present," I call out, not waiting for them to respond as I lead the way inside, stalking after the little blonde devil lover. I don't bother paying attention to whether or not the kid or Red are following me. If they want to learn something, they'll stick close. Just as the last reddish rays in the sky start melting into dusk, I swing the door open to the Light of Lucifer and swagger inside. I haven't made it more than a few steps before someone yelps and some big asshole turns around to point at me.

"Hey! You can't bring that in here, and there's no smoking," he shouts, marching over to me, and I swing the hatchet off my shoulder and point it at him.

"Not a good idea, Lucifer boy." I grin, moving my eyes over the new interior of the church before I rest the weapon against my collarbone again and take a drag off my smoke. "Damn, you guys didn't really put much effort into improving this place when you rebuilt it. Looks just as shitty as it used to."

"Are you a member?" a female voice asks, and I look over at her in her fancy robe and tilt my head to the side.

"Old acquaintance," I reply, looking the black-haired chick over and trying to figure out what kind of body she's hiding under that robe. "I just wanted to see if you knew where one of Lucifer's favorite bitches might be hanging out these days."

"Well, who are you looking for?" she asks, a hint of a blush in her cheeks as she takes a step closer to me.

"Beatrix St. Germain." The name summons a few gasps from the gathered idiots nearby, conversation picking up again, but goth girl's eyes just go wide for a second before a wide smile takes over her face.

"My name is Allisandra, and I'm the High Priestess here at the Light of Lucifer. Why don't you come in and talk with me?" She waves toward the interior, and I glance back over my shoulder to see Red holding the Tupperware container.

"Sure thing," I reply, grabbing the gift from Red to tuck it against my side. Chicks are always a sucker when it comes to flowers and hearts, and while I didn't grab any flowers on the way over, I have to hope the heart makes a good enough impression to get the info we're looking for.

## TEN

## Beneath the Depths of Hell

AFTYN

I blow out my breath and walk away from Lakyn, Daphne, and whatever her name is when I realize he already has another one wrapped around his finger.

It's easy enough to do because once Lakyn realizes that he has another groupie drooling all over him, he tunes out everything else. Hell, he seems to get high off it. The same kind of high that one would usually have to come for, Pops gets from being adored.

'*Maybe Mom was wrong*,' I think irritably as I walk down the hallway and take in the art.

This place isn't so bad.

I haven't seen anything yet that would freak me out and almost everyone I've run into since walking away from the groupie circle has either smiled at me or waved hello.

I run a hand back through my hair as I keep walking. I'm hoping that Pops will forget all about me and maybe leave me here. I'm sure I'll be able to get back to New York somehow and, when I do, I'll send the cops straight to his door.

If they don't get Daphne, then at the very least they'll get him. Something about the way he delights in the deaths of others, the way he commands it... Yeah, there's no way in hell he hasn't done this before himself.

I stop walking and step closer to a picture of some kind of goat-looking thing and raise an eyebrow. I have no idea what the fuck it's supposed to be, but I can totally get down with the naked ladies dancing around it in the picture.

I grit my teeth.

That's probably this bastard's end game, minus the entire goat thing. He's way too fucking vain to look like anything other than himself, though it makes me wonder just how far he'd be able to get in life if I used his precious little hatchet to carve his face off.

My lower lip begins to tremble as I wipe away a tear before it has the chance to fall. I wish Wills has was here. Not only would she have already put Lakyn in his fucking place, she was dying to come here.

And I fucked it all up by killing her goddamn charity case.

The longer that realization settles with me, the more I know that I can't turn Lakyn in. I can't let someone else do to him and Daphne what's fallen on my shoulders. It's my responsibility and I refuse to let Willa's death go unavenged.

"Hey, kid!"

I glance over my shoulder and take a deep breath when I hear Lakyn's shout bounce off the walls.

Before he has a chance to find me, I glance up and down the hallway until I see a door that I know I have no business opening and duck inside, pulling it closed behind me.

---

"FUCK!"

I take a deep breath and grit my teeth as I regain my balance. I've managed to steady myself by placing a hand on the wall and letting it help me down the dark staircase. I almost fell down thinking this would be just another room and, somehow, I doubt that the assholes upstairs would have cared any.

Once I reach the bottom of the steps, I extend my foot forward to tap around. I want to be sure there aren't any more stairs so I don't almost fall do—

"Ow! Fuck!"

I grab my nose with one hand, close the other into a fist, and punch the door that's a few steps away from the bottom of the staircase. I wasn't expecting it and walked right into the fucking thing.

After I've sufficiently managed to hurt my hand as much as my nose, I feel around the door until I find the knob, twist it, and push the door open. It's another pitch-black room. Apparently, these fuckers are watching their electricity bill or something.

Because I don't want any more bumps, bruises, or near-death experiences, I decide it's best to feel around the wall for a light switch, which I manage to find easier than I thought I would.

The lights click on, instantly illuminating the room, and as I look around I'm wondering if I walked into a fucking sex dungeon.

The walls are black, so are the tables that line the right side of the room, and there's a few chairs tipped over on the floor.

I walk over to one and use my foot to move it to the side, shuddering when I see it has some strappy thing attached to it.

*I should probably get sanitized after I leave this damn place.*

Glancing around the room, I take in the rest of it which looks pretty mundane, until I see the small stage-looking thing against the back wall.

There's a large portrait hanging in a black frame that I can't exactly make out from where I'm standing, so I do the rational thing and satisfy my curiosity by closing the gap and taking a look.

*Pretty,* I think with a smirk as I stop in front of the stage.

The woman in the painting has long, blonde hair, big blue eyes, and a smile that would light up a psych ward.

It's weird, though, because the longer I stand here and stare at her, the more I feel like she's staring back.

I never did care for art, but I can appreciate the fine details and hard work that goes into almost anything.

I rub the back of my neck and cast a glance over my shoulder. I don't see any of the creepy crawlies that Pops was so sure still inhabited this place, so I step up on the stage, wrap my hands around the small, metal gate that keeps some space between the portrait and the weirdos upstairs.

Carefully, I lean over the gate and squint when I see a sign under her portrait.

"Filia Satanas."

'*I'll be fucked if I know what that means,*' I think with the shake of my head. '*That's enough of this room.*'

I let go of the gate and turn to walk out of the room when I'm greeted by an extremely unwelcome sight.

Pops, Daphne, and the Priestess chick.

All standing there, staring at me—like I'm some kind of freak for being in here.

At least Daphne and the Priestess are.

Pops is looking past me.

Eyes on the portrait, a carefully crafted mixture of emotions on his face.

Anger.

Hate.

Determination.

Longing.

I watch as he shoves the plastic container toward Daphne without so much as even looking at her. Then he walks straight toward me, hatchet firmly in his hand.

I brace myself, so sure that he's going to try to bury the fucking thing in me, but when he steps up onto the stage, he shoves me aside roughly.

I lose my footing and hit the ground hard, but even with the sudden movement, I'm able to swat the gate away when he yanks it out of its place and tosses it aside.

With a grunt, he pulls his arm back then buries the hatchet in the center of the portrait. The room falls silent with the exception of his heavy breathing and I scoot away from him.

I think this is the first time I've ever seen him show any kind of emotion besides aloofness and annoyance, and I'd be a liar if I said that I didn't feel afraid.

Lakyn reaches for the handle of the hatchet again, and with another grunt drags the blade down the center of the portrait.

He cracks his neck before he pulls it out of the decimated piece of art that was clearly once a thing of pride in this place, then turns on his heel and walks out of the room like the rest of us aren't even here.

I don't know who the person in the portrait was, but obviously he does.

And I have a feeling that we'll all find out at some point.

Whether we want to or not.

## ELEVEN

## Broken Pictures and Promises

DAPHNE

All I can do is stand there as Lakyn storms out of the weird basement. He's not smiling, and although I want to follow him so I can hear the end of the story he was telling us about one of the past head priestesses he knew... I have to see what pissed him off so much. Heading toward the small stage, I glance back at the priestess lady. "What is that?"

"It's— Well, it *was* a painting done by one of our members of a woman named Beatrix." The woman stops beside me as we both stare at the ruined painting. "Beatrix St. Germain is well known here at the Light of Lucifer. She was one of our first head priestesses, and although much of her time here was... contentious, we still recognize her commitment." She sighs heavily, crossing her arms over her stomach. "I wish he hadn't done that."

"Beatrix…" I repeat the name, aware of Aftyn pushing himself up from the ground, but I don't take my eyes away from the canvas. Lakyn buried the hatchet directly in the woman's face, which is obliterated beyond recognition, but I can still see blonde hair.

"Apparently Pops isn't a fan of her."

"*Apparently* she's your aunt," I reply, glancing at Aftyn who just sneers at me.

"I really don't fucking care who she is, or why she's got her own little shrine here."

I shake my head, still not understanding why Aftyn isn't at least a tiny bit excited to have found his father and have him be someone who really lives his life instead of coasting along. Bored and boring. Lakyn doesn't see limits on the world. He doesn't see the rules that society tries to force on everyone. He's just… above it. Free.

And isn't that what we all strive to be?

"Damn," the priestess whispers, turning toward the stairs in a rush, and that's when I hear it.

Screaming. Panic.

*It sounds beautiful.*

"What the fuck is he doing now?" Aftyn growls, stomping over to the door, and I stay right on his heels as he heads up the dark steps, both of us getting closer and closer to the random shouts and panicked cries.

But the closer I get to the door, the more clear the underlying voice becomes. It's Lakyn, and he's shouting… about Beatrix.

"Come on. It's Beatrix. Blonde? Irritating and crazy? Self-professed Satan's favorite? Someone here knows something." Lakyn's voice is loud, echoing down the hall as we step out of the stairwell and move toward the main part of the church, or whatever this place is. Anti-church? I have no fucking idea what Satanists like to call their stuff, but a feminine yelp catches my attention as Lakyn finally comes into view.

He's got a pretty blonde girl tucked against his chest; one arm wrapped across her chest to hold her there. Although the presence of the hatchet so close to her throat is probably doing most of the convincing for her to stay still.

"Listen." Lakyn chuckles, shifting his grip on the hatchet to point it at the people gathered around, moving it in a slow arc. "You have a fucking altar to the bitch downstairs, so that means someone here has a hard dick for Beatrix St. Germain, and all I want to know is where the fuck she's squatting now."

"Let her go!" a man shouts, and Lakyn brings the hatchet back to her throat with a wild grin.

"Come on. Tell me what to do again, Lucifer boy." Lakyn leans down a little, just enough to press a kiss to the girl's hair, and I feel a frisson of jealousy even as the blonde starts crying harder.

Her whimpers are fucking annoying, and I can almost imagine the spray of blood if he cuts the girl. Her heart is definitely racing, blood pressure spiking, and if he slices through the carotid with that sharp as fuck blade... we'll all get a show.

"Excuse me?" the priestess steps forward, her hands out to her sides. "Beatrix hasn't come to visit us in a long time, but I do have some people I can call to ask about her. Would you like me to do that?"

"Go ahead," he said, shifting to face the woman. "We'll wait."

"Please don't kill me." The blonde girl pressed against him is dressed in all black, and Lakyn leans his cheek against the top of her head, shushing her softly.

"Don't start begging yet," he mock whispers, more than loud enough for everyone to hear. "You'll spoil the effect."

"Everyone calm down, please. Just take your seats. Everything will be fine." The priestess doesn't seem scared of Lakyn at all as she moves closer. If anything, she seems drawn to him—which I can understand— but Lakyn has already had me trim the herd once for this road trip, and I won't hesitate to do it again. When the bitch lays her hand on his arm, I'm tempted to slice it off, but Lakyn just tilts his head at her and she drops it. "Will you please let Brittany go? I'm more than happy to show you my office and I'll make the calls. Then... perhaps we can talk about some other things?"

*Bitch.*

"What do you say, Brittany?" Lakyn asks, leaning down to speak right against her ear. "Do you believe your priestess?"

"Allisandra h-has the m-member rosters," the blonde girl stutters, sniffling loudly. "Sh-she'd know."

"Fantastic." Moving the hatchet, Lakyn grabs Brittany's arm and spins her away from him like he's dancing. She quickly loses her balance from the force of it, stumbling into one of the people crowded near the pews, but they manage to keep her from falling. "Lead on."

"Of course. This way." Allisandra gestures toward the other side of the room, heading toward a door against the opposite wall, but a tall man stops her.

"Priestess, are you sure this is—"

"He's a friend of Beatrix St. Germain, and he's our guest," she replies, pointing toward the stage at the front of the room. "Why don't you lead service this evening, Roderick?"

"But, Priestess…" The man trails off, glaring at Lakyn, who just offers a grin as he adjusts the hatchet on his shoulder.

"Go lead the service, Roderick." Allisandra's voice turns hard, intense, and I have to give her some credit. She's the top bitch in this place, and that has to mean something since they're all supposed to be a bunch of Satan worshipers—although none of them seem very intimidating.

"Shoo." Lakyn flicks his fingers at the man, grinning when the idiot balls his hands into fists and storms off.

"Sorry about that, he's still so eager to prove himself." The head priestess shrugs gently and leads them through a door and down a short hall into an office, which looks remarkably… average. No giant devil statue, no big pentagram drawn in blood on the wall. It's pretty disappointing, especially since Lakyn had originally planned to offer these idiots the heart she'd carved out of Gladys' chest.

At least the Tupperware will keep it relatively fresh for now. Until they can think of something fun to do with it.

Allisandra takes the chair behind the desk, scooting it in before she opens the lid of the laptop and starts typing something. Her gaze flicks up toward Lakyn. "So... you really know Beatrix St. Germain?"

I lean against the wall just inside the door, watching Lakyn as he stares at the priestess, a strange expression passing over his face for a moment before his smirk returns.

"Yeah, we used to be really close." Lakyn rests the hatchet on the back of one of the chairs meant for guests. "She's just always had... different priorities."

"Lucifer's path isn't the right journey for everyone, but I've always believed Beatrix St. Germain saw things far beyond what others at the Light of Lucifer could comprehend." Allisandra licks her lips, basically eye-fucking Lakyn in front of us. "She's been an inspiration to many women seeking to gain the rank of High Priestess."

"Chicks like you?" Aftyn asks, rolling his eyes as he leans his shoulder against the door frame.

"Ignore the kid, he's still in that 'angry at the world' phase," Lakyn says, tilting his chin toward the computer. "You mentioned you had some people you could call?"

"Of course." Allisandra smiles, and it takes actual effort not to roll my eyes too at the woman's blatant flirting.

OVER THIRTY MINUTES LATER, I'm sitting on the floor, bored to fucking tears, and so sick of listening to the priestess talk on the phone. Lakyn is in one of the guest chairs, his feet kicked up on the corner of her desk, the hatchet in his lap and a cigarette between his lips.

The only bit of fun was when Aftyn had tried to light up and Lakyn threw a pen at him and told him there was no smoking inside. I'd smiled at that, but Lakyn hadn't spared me a glance, and my smile had disappeared just as fast.

"You're sure?" Allisandra asks, flashing a bright smile at Lakyn from across the desk. "Got it. West on I-40? And then 66? Wonderful. Thank you so much, Carlos."

"Finally got an answer?" Lakyn drops his feet to the floor, leaning forward to brace an elbow on the desk.

"Apparently she's in the western part of Arizona in the Mojave Desert off Route 66. I guess there's an old community out there that she's joined." Setting her cell phone down, Allisandra folds her hands in front of her. "I understand that you want to go see Beatrix… but I was wondering if you'd be interested in coming back here?"

"Why would I do that?" Jabbing out his cigarette on a coaster, Lakyn stands up, swinging the hatchet at his side.

*Yes. Please kill her.*

"There aren't enough truly committed members here. Not like Beatrix used to be... and not like you."

"I've never been a member here." Lakyn chuckles, shoving the guest chair out of his way so he can step away from her desk. "Never been much of a joiner. People tend to follow *me*, not the other way around."

"That's exactly what I mean!" Pushing up from her seat, Allisandra suddenly sounds a lot more desperate. "You could be a leader here. Perhaps you could even bring back ideas from Beatrix's journeys on the path of Lucifer?"

Lakyn sucks his teeth, looking the woman over. "Yeah... that's not going to happen."

"But you could—"

"Like I said before, I'm not a follower, and I sure as fuck don't run errands for Trixie, or Lucifer." He shrugs, swinging the hatchet onto his shoulder again. "And I'd stay, but a crown doesn't do anything for my hair."

"I just see so much potential in what you could do here at the Light of Lucifer. With you leading us, we could be truly great." Moving around the desk, the priestess stops short of actually touching him again, and I'm curious about what's going through Lakyn's mind when he suddenly grins.

"You know, Beatrix is one of my best friends, and we're on our way to go see her. Why don't you just come with me? That way you could hear whatever you want to hear from the mouth of Satan's number one bitch herself." He leans in, so close that for a second I'm convinced he's going to kiss her, but he stops short. "I know how much you want to meet her."

"I… I don't know if I can just—"

"Fine." Sighing, Lakyn turns away from her and I scramble up from the floor as Aftyn stands up in the hallway, tucking his phone into his pocket.

"Wait!" she raises her voice, looking nervous as fuck, and I feel a small smile spread across my lips as she toys with the idea. "Okay. I'll come with you."

"Take off the robe." Lakyn lifts his eyebrows when she doesn't move, and after a moment she reaches down and gathers the fabric in her hands, pulling it up. Higher and higher, it just reveals more skin, and then more.

*Naked? What the fuck?*

Laughing, Lakyn turns to look at Aftyn, gesturing toward Allisandra as she drops the robe onto the desk. "Check that out. Some things never fucking change."

"That's what the dungeon is for downstairs?" he asks, and Lakyn grins.

"I was actually telling that story while you were off exploring. This place can be fun when the right people are present."

"I'd still like to hear the end of the story," I say, but he only looks at me for a second before his intense blue eyes are back on the priestess, which just makes me want to hurt the bitch more.

*If she thinks she can replace me, she has another thing coming.*

"You have clothes here?" Lakyn looks her over again as she nods. "Well, then I think you should get dressed. We need to get back on the road."

"Okay, just… um… give me a few minutes. I'll tell Roderick that I'm going to find Beatrix with you." Allisandra is almost out the door, still completely naked, when she stops and turns to look at him. "Can I have your name now?"

"Not yet."

She hesitates again, but then she nods and walks back toward the main church area. Lakyn steps into the hall and both he and Aftyn watch her walk away.

Lakyn drops his hand on Aftyn's shoulder, chuckling. "We'll get your dick wet before this road trip is over. My treat."

"Party favor?" I ask and this time Lakyn grins at me.

"What's a better party favor than the Head Priestess of Beatrix's old stomping grounds?"

# TWELVE

## Ghost of Bitchmas Past

### LAKYN

Now that I've finally got some direction on where Trixie has been hiding her rotten gash for the past twenty or so odd years, I'm in a much better mood.

The kid still seems to be sucking on sour grapes, and had he not been mine, I would have given him something better to suck on, but *c'est la vie*.

I clear my throat as I tune out the two in the back of the truck. Granted, one of them is poking at the other, literally and figuratively speaking, though I can totally get the fun in that. Once I've got a chick all nice and tied up, I tend to fuck with them for a little while before the grand finale.

Glancing into the rearview, I chuckle and shake my head as Red pushes the new head emo girl's gag further into her mouth.

"Careful not to choke her on that. Trixie doesn't like to play with dead things."

*For the most part anyway,* I muse to myself as thoughts of her fucking Basil's corpse come flooding back.

I shift in the seat as a way to keep my dick from getting hard from the memory, then begin to chew the inside of my mouth thoughtfully. The best thing to do is probably listen to some tunes right now since it'll help drown them out even more, and it might even perk the kid up.

Leaning over, I press the power button and then the scan button to let the radio search for something. I have no idea what the fuck channels she had these set to, but I'm sure I'll find something good at some point.

*Bingo.*

A grin that spreads over half my face takes over as I raise the volume. I begin to tap my fingers along the steering wheel as the temp picks up.

*"Stars live in the evening…"*

The kid immediately reaches over to shut the radio off, and I slap his hand away.

"Tsk, tsk," I say to him as I raise a finger. "Daddy's listening to his favorite song."

When he scowls, I smirk and go back to humming along. *Pretty Baby* is something that I've loved for years before I met Trixie, but when I met that little demon spawn, the song took on more meaning.

Raking a hand back through my hair, I begin to bop my head along to the beat as I reach into the visor for another smoke. I'd offer him one, but since he's being a little shit, he'll have to learn to survive off the fumes for a while.

When the song ends, I let out a dramatic sigh. There's not a goddamn thing that can compare to that song. The noble thing to do would be to let the kid pick the next song, but…

"You like Springsteen?" I ask as *Born in the USA* comes on. He doesn't look at me, doesn't shake his head or nod; hell, he doesn't even blink, so I shrug and raise the volume another notch.

Maybe he's finally understanding that I know what good music is and he's accepting it. Of course, he could have had an aneurysm and died for all I know. Not like it matters; he's only going with me because he's my in with Trixie.

I'll finally be able to show the little bitch that I did something she could never do and that even her goat god would fucking choose me over her any day.

Not that it would matter to her.

She's probably so far gone now that she won't even recognize me.

I haven't changed at all.

I've aged like fine fucking wine and taste just as sweet. Which is something I'm going to make damn sure she notices before I leave.

*Twenty goddamn years,* I think irritably as I grip the steering wheel and press down on the gas. *I've dealt with her fucking charity case. Housed him, clothed him, let him experience me every single goddamn night and she probably won't think it's worth a damn anymore. And to think she's been under my nose this entire time. Back in fucking Arizona.*

"Whoa, Lakyn!" the kid shouts from the passenger seat.

I glance at him sharply, but when I see that he has one of his hands on the interior roof of the car, and the other plastered against the dashboard, I turn my attention back to the road in front of me.

"Whoops!" I say cheerfully as I quickly swerve to avoid crashing into the car in front of us. I pull up next to the frightened couple, give them a one-fingered salute, and drive around them.

"Are you crazy? You almost killed us!" he shouts, his voice cracking slightly.

"You know," I begin conversationally as I light my smoke. Taking a drag, I inhale deeply, then let a billow of smoke out of the corner of my mouth. "That's *exactly* what your Aunt Trixie said to me once. It's a great story actually. So, Ichabod—" I grit my teeth when Red's fingers suddenly dig around the side of my seat. Seems she's damn determined to hang onto my every word. I clear my throat, lay an elbow back into her arm to move her, then take another drag, "Anyway, the last time I was at Satan's Party House, there was a new girl there too. Jizzy or some shit I think her name was. Well, Ichabod thought it would be the right thing to do to stay behind and pay homage to Trixie by helping them pick up the pieces of what she left behind. Man, if you lived in this area, you would have heard about what she did. I was damn proud of that girl for finally burning that place to the ground like she always said she would."

Aftyn shifts uncomfortably in the seat next to me and I chuckle.

"Of course, he doesn't even know how to wipe his own ass, so it was up to me to get him the fuck out of there before they made him hail their goat thing. The thing is, I knew he wouldn't leave with me again, so I found Trixie. Know where she was? At the old junkie house," I state with an eye roll. "But yeah, I found her, she went back with me and we got him the fuck out of there. See? I'm pretty cool once you get to know me. I saved a life once."

I grin at the kid who's staring at me like I'm insane, but he doesn't get it obviously. I'm an honest man with particular tastes and I like to have fun.

What the hell would life be like if someone couldn't tell the truth and have fun? With their kinks or otherwise? Boring as fuck, and I refuse to partake in anything that bores me.

Which is why we're on our way to find Trixie.

"Wanna know how I met her?" I ask glancing at him again.

"It almost sounds like you've got an out of control crush, Pops," he replies carefully.

"Me? Not at all," I reply with a laugh. "I just think that if you're going to meet your auntie, you may want a little background info is all."

"Am I going to be able to stop you from telling me?" he asks, his tone going back to the miserable little bastard that watched his bestie get whacked.

"Nope!"

I grin at him before I turn my eyes toward the road and take another pull from my smoke. I glance down at it and grunt as I flick it out of the window and light a new one.

"Well, I was at a bar in Albuquerque one night, *The Blue Devil Saloon*; you should check it out sometime. I was listening to tunes, picking out my fuck toy for the night, when the bartender came over and told me that someone with terrible taste in music was pissed off over my playlist. Some people, am I right?" I scoff with an eye roll. The kid opens his mouth to say something, but since it was a rhetorical question, I keep going. "Anyway, a few seconds later, I find myself face to face with this tiny blonde that had the perkiest, tight little body I've ever seen in my goddamn life. But you know what got me to stay in the seat that night?"

"Psychosis?" he grumbles.

I reach over and smack him one. When he gives me a dirty stare, I smirk and continue my little anecdote. "What I saw in those big, blue eyes of hers. It was like looking into the eyes of evil and sheer insanity all at once, and I'd never seen that before. I knew she'd be much more fun to play with than anyone else I'd take back to the hotel I was staying in for the night."

I take a deep breath as the thoughts of how Trixie looked that night come flooding back to me. So fucking young, clearly not old enough to be in a place like that, and casing me like *I* was the prey instead of her.

"Hey, before you keep going, can you be anymore cliché?" he asks. I glance at him and when I see the smirk on his face, mine drops instantly.

"Meaning?" I ask, knowing I'm not going to like the answer.

"Picking up a blonde with blue eyes in a bar? I thought that the Great Lakyn Meyer would have been cooler than that. Guess you're just a legend in your own head."

I let out a good-natured laugh. Apparently, he thinks his attempt at a barb is going to hurt my feelings, but I'm not done yet.

"Shut your mouth and listen. You may learn something, little boy," I reply smugly as I accelerate toward the car in front of us. When he lets out a strangled scream, I swerve around them at the last moment.

Glancing in the rearview, I see that Red is still nursing her superficial wounds, but she's gone back to taunting Satan's Next Great Wannabe Bitch so at least she'll keep out of trouble for now.

"We introduce ourselves to each other as responsible adults tend to do." I say, taking a swipe at his childish bullshit. "I struck up as much small talk as I could with her, but honestly all I could think about was how tight her pussy had to be and how I bad I wanted to stretch it out, you know? Oh, this is a *great* song!" I say, dialing up the volume again. I was never a huge fan of Whitesnake but watching that redhead roll around on the hood of the car was always nice. "Let me cut to the chase of this story because I kind of feel like I'm dragging it out."

"Coulda fooled me," the kid mutters.

I cast a sidelong glance in his direction, "Was your mother this much of a whiny bitch too?"

When he gives me a death stare, I shrug. I'm genuinely curious because fuck if I remember her.

"God, I hate you," he says through grit teeth.

"Take a number," I reply breezily. *Where the fuck was I? Oh yeah, the good part.* "She ended up talking me into going back to her church. It's where we had our first party favor together." A wistful smile creeps over my lips as finally, a memory of Trixie makes me smile instead of sets my teeth on edge. "You know that little underground room you wandered into? That's where we had her. I guess Trixie was on the eve of becoming some kind of superhero for her goat and she needed a sacrifice or some shit. I don't know how it works; I never cared really, but there was free pussy to be had and she did the dirty work of getting rid of her, so I figured why the fuck not? Anyway, I fucked the party favor senseless. To the point where I think she forgot her own goddamn name. Trixie played with her pussy while she watched us and even though I had already promised her that I wouldn't fuck her that night, the thought never left me." I pause to take another drag of my smoke before I flick it out the window and finish the story. "She slit her throat after she had me come into some chalice thing. Then we went and knelt by that banister thing where her picture was hanging and she said some weird prayer thing, drank the essence of life, and that was it. We somehow became tied together forever."

When the kid doesn't say anything, I glance over to see what the fuck he's doing, then blow out my breath in exasperation. I reach over and unclip his seatbelt, then remove the child-lock on his door. Seems that I lost him somewhere between a hard, vicious fuck and a sacrifice and he's been trying to get out of the truck.

"Go ahead and jump," I dare him with a smirk. Actually, wait."

I crack my neck as I grip the steering wheel tightly and press down on the gas pedal as far as it will go, lurching the truck forward and intense speed.

"Woo!" I shout out as my hair begins to whip around my face. It's actually quite exhilarating, but when I glance at the waste of a fuck, he looks like he's about to piss his pants.

Rolling my eyes, I ease up on the speed and shrug.

"Thought you wanted to jump? If you're going to take a tumble, may as well make it a good one. Granted, I'm not one for cleaning up roadkill so if you thought I was going to stop and see if you were okay, it wasn't going to happen. Now why don't you buckle that seatbelt back up, behave for a few more hours, and smile at your Aunt Trixie when you meet her, eh? She's gonna be confused enough as it is when I show up."

The kid uses the back of his hand to wipe the tears from his face and I sigh loudly. How? How the fuck is it possible that this scared, passive aggressive little shit came out of my sac?

*Ah well.*

Taking a deep breath, I lean my elbow on the window frame and keep driving. We'll catch up to Trixie soon, and when we do, things will finally fucking go my way for once.

## THIRTEEN

## Blonde Damsels and Demons

AFTYN

I don't know why I got back in this fucking truck.

Lakyn is a complete and total asshole and all I want right now is to get the hell away from him. Unfortunately, the urge to literally jump out of a moving car just seemed to entertain him, and as I rub the sleeve of my shirt over my cheek again, I can hear him chuckling under his breath.

All of this is just too much.

It hasn't even been a whole day with him yet and I've already seen my father stomp an old guy's face in and wrestle that priestess chick into the back of the SUV after the sun went down. Honestly, if I was smart, I would have just walked away right then. Right into the middle of the fucking desert where at least I wouldn't have to think about the psycho bitch in the backseat gutting an old woman to get to her heart… or the way she'd shoved that knife into Willa.

*Willa.*

Every time I think about her being gone, *really* gone, it makes my stomach twist and my throat go stiff and then it's impossible to keep my goddamn eyes from leaking.

But how am I not supposed to think about her?

We're in *her* car. I've got her fucking hair tie around my wrist and I'm sitting where she was this morning. Still alive, and beautiful, and completely pissed at me because I killed her charity case. If I could fix it, I would. I'd do whatever it takes just to have her sitting next to me, glaring at me, furious and ready to drive a knife into someone else because she could never bring herself to really hurt me.

That's just how Willa is. *Was.*

A painful lump catches in my throat and it won't go back down no matter how hard I try to swallow, but when it finally reaches my mouth it bursts over my lips in the strangest groan I've ever made. Some mix between pain and rage—and I feel both.

"Put your damn seatbelt on, and if you throw up in here, I'm gonna smack you again," Lakyn says casually, the smoke drifting out of the corner of his mouth. A fragment of it swirls around the dash of the SUV before the wind eventually rips it out his window, and I wonder if a cigarette will help this intense pressure in my chest.

Leaning forward, I grab the carton of cigarettes Lakyn brought with him and take out a fresh pack. My hands are shaking as I tear the plastic off, and I rip the cardboard trying to get the top flipped up, but eventually I manage to get one between my teeth. It takes five or six flicks of the lighter to finally get it to light and then I take the longest drag I can, trying to pull in as much nicotine as possible in an effort to hold back whatever feeling is rising inside me.

I don't know what it is, but I know it's bad, and I don't want to feel it.

Fuck, I don't want to feel *anything*.

I crack the window to let some of the smoke escape and the increased roar of the wind rushing past the car manages to muffle the whimpers of the priestess in the back and whatever shit Daphne keeps saying to her. The white noise, along with the tease of nicotine in my veins, seems to be helping a little—or it could be the fact that I'm bent forward over my legs, practically in the fetal position as all the insane shit Lakyn said keeps spinning through my head.

That pretty blonde with the blue eyes in the picture, the same one he buried his goddamn hatchet in, was apparently his partner in crime for a while. Just like Willa was for me. Only Trixie used Lakyn to complete some weird satanic shit, while Willa did everything *for* me.

Even though I tried so hard to hide it, she'd always known what a raging bitch my mother was. She'd seen right through my act, but she hadn't seen me as weak. Instead, she'd seen the potential inside me, the violence waiting just under the surface for someone to unlock it—and Willa was my key. She was the one who told me it was okay to want the bitch dead, that it was okay to do it. She was the one who helped me, who gave me a place to live afterward, who kept me fed and my clothes washed.

She was… everything.

And now she's gone.

But Lakyn's blonde demon is still alive somewhere out in this fucking desert, waiting for Lakyn to bring her another party favor for another round of sex and murder and drinking his cum, or whatever the fuck he was rambling about.

How is *that* fair? Why does he let Trixie live, but take Willa away from me? Why does he get to keep his partner in crime while telling the bitch in the backseat to murder mine?

*Fuck me.* They even look alike. His demon and my Willa.

Am I that much like him? Am I going to turn out the same way? Will I just grow old filling my time with casual violence because my life is so goddamn empty that the only thing I can fill it with is blood?

*Maybe.*

Without Willa anything is possible.

She was the only thing keeping me whole. Keeping me human. Keeping me functioning on the day to day and I never even fucking recognized it. I didn't even see just how central she'd become until Lakyn snuffed out her light with a flick of his hand. When I saw her on the floor… my whole damn universe went dark, and it's hard to believe it was only this afternoon. How many hours? Eight, nine? No time at all, but without a center everything is just spinning out of control. My feet aren't on the ground anymore because she was gravity, and air, and light.

I don't think I can live without her here.

But she's gone.

She's actually fucking gone.

"FUCK!" I shout, pain rocketing up my arm as I realize I just punched the goddamn dash hard enough to split the skin over the knuckle of my ring finger, but the bright flash of red on my skin just makes me remember Willa at the end. Dead. Throat slit, belly torn open, and covered in blood. So much red, and for once it didn't bring me any excitement. There had just been an emptiness, and now that's what I am. I'm empty.

I'm so fucking empty that I think my chest is going to cave in.

"Kid, you need to calm down." Lakyn turns the music down enough that I can hear the wheezing breaths grating in and out of my lungs over the rush of wind outside the truck. "What the hell is wrong with you?"

"You took Willa from me!" My voice cracks as I yell over the fucking music and the road noise and everything else that suddenly feels like it's pressing in on me, crushing me.

"Technically Red is the one who—"

"SHUT UP!" I roar. Bracing my hands on the dash, I try to breathe normally, but I'm staring into the floorboard of Willa's fucking SUV at the smudged ash from a cigarette marring the floor mat that had been absolutely pristine before this damn trip.

The trip I pushed her to take.

"What's going on?" Daphne asks, and I know she's facing forward again even though I refuse to look.

"Kid is freaking out over the chick you killed. He might actually pop a blood vessel at this point." Lakyn reaches over and flicks the side of my forehead. "Check out that vein throbbing. Don't think you got this bullshit drama act from me."

*I hate you.*

Another broken sound tumbles from my lips and this time I don't even have the capacity to try and stop it. Nothing matters without Willa. I got her killed because I wanted to meet my father, and for the first time in my life my mother was actually right about something—he isn't worth knowing at all.

I didn't get a single decent thing from either of the people that brought me into this world and I never fucking asked to be born. Tears are burning my eyes, my nose is running, and I know I'm shaking like a damn bomb about to explode. I can feel the rage welling up inside me, and I hate that it just proves I'm exactly like the bastard that fathered me... because the only thing I want right now is to feel their blood coating my hands.

*I'm going to kill you.*

*I'm going to kill both of you.*

*Then I'm going to find a way to join Willa.*

"Stop the car. I need to get out." I force the words out, and I hear the irritating sound of Lakyn sucking his teeth.

"Not really in the cards, kid."

"NOW!" I shout, and for a second I'm so desperate for some fucking breathing room that I try to figure out if I could survive a fall out of the SUV... but I know we're going too fast. The road would shred my clothes and my skin in no time, and then I'd be too damn weak to drive that knife through Daphne's flesh or bury Lakyn's hatchet in his throat.

"First of all, don't tell me what the fuck to do, kid. Second—"

Something in me snaps and I lunge for the steering wheel, jerking it to the side. Daphne yelps and I hear a horn blare just as I catch headlights out of the corner of my eye. We narrowly miss them—mostly because the other car slammed on their breaks—but then Lakyn clocks me in the face with his elbow and a starburst of pain explodes beside my eye. I end up against the door, holding onto the headrest as he swerves the SUV back onto the road.

I'm expecting him to hit me again, or try to kill me, or *anything* except what he actually does.

He laughs.

With that bullshit fucking grin on his face.

"Damn, kid... maybe you do have some balls after all." Shaking his head, Lakyn cracks his neck and then pops another cigarette between his teeth, lighting it as he points out the windshield. "Six miles to the next town. Think you can suppress your urge to crash the car for ten minutes?"

I keep my mouth shut, rubbing the sore place near my temple as I try to figure out if I'm going to have a blackeye by morning or not. Not like it fucking matters, but the last thing I want is to look like Lakyn beat the shit out of me when we get wherever we're going. Somehow, I just know it would make him happy —and I only want him to suffer. Clenching my teeth hard enough to hear them creaking inside my skull, I pop open the pack of cigarettes just to have something to keep me busy for the next miserable minutes before I can at least walk away from him for a little bit.

I just need some fucking silence, some air that I don't have to share with the two people who ruined my life by killing the only good thing in it.

Just as I light it, taking that first puff to dull the edge of my rage a little, I remember what Daphne said to Willa when she had the knife pressed against her throat. Right here. In this seat. It wasn't just a random knife… it was the knife Willa used on that guy we found at the park. When she chose to kill that random couple *instead* of me.

Turning around in my seat, I find Daphne with one leg extended across the backseat, her back against the door as she watches the priestess that I know hasn't moved. I can't see her, but she's bound with rope and gagged with a sock and more duct tape than I really think is necessary.

But I don't give a shit what they do to the goth princess, I'm just wondering if she'll distract them enough to let their guard down so I can kill one—or both—of them tonight.

"Hey," I say, blowing smoke into the backseat, and I actually manage to smile a little when I see Daphne flinch as the cloud hits her in the face. "I want that knife you took off the couple in the woods."

"Why?"

My rage ratchets up another couple of notches and so I take a long drag, letting it soak in before I blow the smoke right at her. "Because I want it."

"It's not the only knife I have," she says, tilting her head a bit as she narrows her eyes at me.

"Then it shouldn't fucking matter if you give it to me," I snap.

"Fine." Rolling her eyes, she grabs her backpack from the floor and digs through it, slapping the handle of the knife onto my open palm a few seconds later. Just as I wrap my fingers around it, she takes out another one, but this blade is folded in until she swipes her thumb over the side and it swings out, clicking into place.

It's black, and although it's shorter than the one in my hand, I can tell it's very sharp—whereas the one I'm holding is more than a little well-used. The guy had it with his fishing gear, but I'm oddly comforted by the fact that Willa cleansed any lingering residue of fish off of it by stabbing it into the asshole thirty-something times. Somehow that tiny bit of knowledge makes it easier to swallow that Willa ended up gutted by the same knife. Daphne leans back against the seat and I realize I've been staring at her when she says, "See something you like?"

"No." I'm sure my face shows how disgusted I am by her bullshit attempt at flirting before I turn around and set Willa's knife on my thigh. The blade belongs with me. It's tied to both of us, and even though it looks clean... Willa's blood still touched it. This thin piece of metal took her life, and so, in a way, it's my last connection to her. More powerful than the hair tie around my wrist, and a hell of a lot more helpful.

"Think you can actually use that?" Lakyn asks, glancing over at me.

"Wouldn't be the first time, Pops."

He just laughs, low and quiet, and the way the lights from the dash cast his face in shadow makes him look creepy as fuck. "We'll see about that." Flicking his cigarette out the window, Lakyn takes the next exit. "I think we'll try out our party favor and then get some rest before we hit the road again to go find your auntie in the daylight."

*Whatever.*

It's hard to believe this town exists because it's surrounded by so much empty black. I can't see shit more than ten feet off the road, but in the distance the light pollution forms a bubble of gray haze around this random pitstop of civilization somewhere in Arizona. Unfortunately, Lakyn isn't headed toward the center of town, he's slowing down and I already know where he's headed.

There's an absolute shit hole of a motel ahead, with a dismal looking gas station a little beyond it, and he proves me right when he swings into the almost empty parking lot.

"Only the best for you, eh Pops?" I ask, and he sighs.

"Why don't you start crying over your dead girlfriend that you never had the balls to fuck while I go in and get us a room?" Lakyn's gaze barely brushes me before he leans into the back. "Keep the party favor quiet, Red. We don't want anyone spoiling our fun."

"Of course!" she answers, all chipper and batshit fucking crazy.

I hate them both so much, but I just tighten my grip on the handle of the knife, imagining what it will feel like to plunge it into her belly and watch the light leave her eyes.

"Right," Lakyn mutters, swinging his legs out of the SUV. He slams the door behind him, stretching his back out for a few seconds before he walks inside the dim motel office to talk to the sweaty-looking fuck behind the counter.

"Don't worry, I'll keep you safe," Daphne whispers, and I glance back to see her leaned over the seat talking to the priestess.

*What. The. Fuck.*

I'm tempted to tell the woman the truth—that she's definitely going to die, probably horribly—but Willa never got a real warning, so why should I help out the devil-worshiping wannabe? Nope. If she's dumb enough to believe that psycho, then she deserves whatever Daphne will do to her.

It's not like I've ever been a hero anyway.

I was always the villain in my mother's world, and I turned out to be the villain in Willa's too.

But what should I have expected? I'm the spawn of an abusive whore and a bastard named Lakyn Meyer and the only thing I have waiting for me in my future is violence and blood and death, and… honestly, that doesn't bother me as much as it probably should.

As long as two of the bodies on that path are Daphne and my father, then I'll walk into Hell with my head held high and I'll just have to hope that Willa will be there waiting for me when I finally arrive.

## FOURTEEN

## Only the Lonely

ICHABOD

I've cleaned the house twice now.

I've taken a nap.

I've made myself lunch, then dinner.

I went to check on the sludge that Willa became before I poured another half-gallon of acid into the tub.

And now, I've spent the past few hours laying on the couch in the living room staring at the ceiling.

The house always seems different when Lakyn isn't in it, and while it usually bothers me, this time I know it's for the best.

I'll actually be anticipating his arrival instead of dreading it because Bea will be with him.

I let out a chuckle as a wide smile creeps across my lips. Running a hand over my face, I think about how happy I'll be once the three of us are together again.

*I can't wait.*

I fold my hands behind my neck and let out a breath. I know that putting my faith in Lakyn doing the right thing for once could be seriously misplaced, but he promised, and he always follows through on those. No matter how many times he has to try to get it right.

But that's the thing about Lakyn Meyer.

He may be a narcissistic psychopath that only cares about getting his rocks off with the closest hole that he can stick his dick into; once he gives you his word, it's his bond.

*I should have asked him long he thought this would take.*

I close my eyes and sigh.

That's the only downfall of having to wait for something as magical as being reunited with Bea; the not knowing when she'll walk in the front door.

I turn on my side and reach for the remote control. Maybe flipping mindlessly through some channels will help get my mind off things for a while.

After going through every channel that we have, on the second go, I settle on *Psycho*. It's always been a favorite of Lakyn's, and he even once made me roleplay the shower scene before he violently violated me.

The only reason I agreed to it was because I was hoping he would have slipped and stabbed me to death, but he's a tricky fellow and knows exactly when to stop before he goes too far.

I roll my eyes as I set the remote control down as Norman Bates checks in Marion then do my best not to fall asleep.

I've been so wired all fucking day, and now that I'm feeling a little relaxed, my body wants to recharge.

And I think I'll let it.

Because when I open my eyes again, Beatrix might be here.

## FIFTEEN

## Rise of the Jackal pt. 1

AFTYN

Lakyn made us all walk into the room ahead of him. Then he kicked the door closed and tossed Allisandra on the bed like a bag of trash before stretching his arms over his head.

"So, this is where things *finally* start to get fun," he begins as he turns slightly to put the chain in place, then flips the lock. My jaw tenses as I watch him settle down in a chair beside a round table and then tilts his head as he grins at each of us in turn. "*You*"—he declares when his eyes fall on me again—"are going to prove to me that you are who you claim to be."

The knife burns a hole in my pocket. Once we got out of the car to shuffle into the room, I knew it would be best if I put it away until the right moment and Lakyn seems to think that this is it.

"And how would you like me to do that, Pops?" I ask through gritted teeth. Another wave of anger crashes over me as Willa's mangled body enters my mind. How she didn't even stand a chance because she was blindsided by Daphne, and how I wasn't even given the opportunity to save her. *I should have tried harder.*

"Simple," he says as he sits back in the chair and grins at me. "Show me what you've got."

I furrow my brow in confusion until he turns his eyes toward the bed. When Allisandra notices that now everyone in the room is staring at her, she begins to buck and scream. The problem is that being tied up as tightly as she is won't allow her to get far. And having a gag shoved almost down her throat muffles the sound of her fear.

"Even you can't be that fucking sick," I snap at him. I have no issues when it comes to fucking a fine piece of ass like Allisandra whether she wants it or not— because once I go to work she'll like it either way— and I don't care about having an audience, but having my own father watch us is too much for even me to bear.

Lakyn shakes his head as he gets to his feet. I tense up when he walks straight for me, grabs me roughly by the elbow and throws me onto the bed next to our 'party favor.'

"Tell you what," he says as he leans down, his fists firmly placed on the mattress, "I'll give you a choice. You either show me that you're my kid or I'll gut you like Red there did your little pal."

The mention of what happened to Willa flips something inside of me. It was the same thing I felt when we crept into Mom's house for the last time. When I knew that everything would be okay again because by the time we left, she would be gone and never able to hurt me again. And even though I've been carrying it with me since it happened, it's hearing from *him* that brings all of the emotions to a boil inside of me again.

*Don't freak out.*

*Don't lose control.*

*Show him what you showed Mom.*

I reach into my pocket and pull the knife out. The one still stained with Willa's blood; the one that I'll soon coat with theirs before I turn it on myself and open my own throat so I can be with my best friend again.

I close my eyes for a moment and tell myself to show him what he's looking for and a little more.

Using my foot, I swat his hands away from the bed as I push myself up to my elbows and look at the captive next to me.

I run a hand back through my hair and push myself off the bed to take my jacket off. I can smell the fear on her because she thinks she knows what's going to happen. She thinks I'm just going to fuck her, and maybe Pops, then we'll let her go, but a witness is never a good thing to leave by the wayside.

I push Lakyn out of the way when I get to the foot of the bed. I want Allisandra's fear to fuel me as much as I know Willa's did to Daphne. Not that she had the chance to be afraid. She got attacked when she wasn't ready for it, because if she had been, it wouldn't have been her that died.

I take a deep breath and crack my neck, refusing to let another tear fall. Now is the time that I get to avenge my best friend and I'm going to do my darndest to make it happen.

"I'm already bored," Lakyn deadpans and I turn to glare at him for a moment. It makes him chuckle; everything that seems to bother everyone in this world, makes that bastard smile.

*Deep breath.*

*He's not important.*

*Nothing is except for this moment.*

I pull my shirt over my head and toss it onto the floor. Behind me, I can hear Lakyn shuffle away. A moment later, I hear the sound of the chair he was sitting in creak as he sits down, followed by the sound of another cigarette being lit.

"Come here, Red," he says to Daphne. "Come sit with me and let's see what he's got."

Another creak which I'm assuming is the table and all that's left is for me to follow through. I don't know why I feel the desperate need inside of me to prove myself to Lakyn, but I know there's no other option left.

I reach for my belt and undo the buckle. Before I reach for my zipper, I retrieve the knife from my pocket and toss it onto the bed. It's a dangerous move since either Lakyn or Daphne could easily swipe it and shank me with it, but that would mean that I'd get to be with Willa sooner rather than later, so I wouldn't give a fuck. My only regret would be that they'd still be standing when I bled out. *Focus.*

I lean down like my father did and use my fists to push into the mattress. I want Allisandra's eyes on me. I want her to see the intent in my eyes, I want her to fucking cry for Willa, and I want her to hurt as much as I do.

"Cigarette number two," Lakyn announces in a bored tone. *Flick. Inhale, exhale.*

I stand back up to my full height and pull my zipper down, shove my jeans to my ankles, then step out of them.

Slipping a hand into the fly of my boxers, I give my dick a couple of tugs. Fucking with an audience? No problem. Being watched and judged by my father? New territory.

"Are you gonna get this going before I become old or do you need Red here to fluff you up?" Lakyn asks loudly.

*Ignore him.*

*Deep breath.*

*Nothing matters.*

*Only Willa.*

As soon as my dick starts to get hard, I grab the knife off the bed and climb on. The fair thing to do would be to cut her restraints, to give her a chance, but many late night card games with Wills taught me that fair can be boring.

Some of those nights would turn into us getting high or drunk. She'd let me finger fuck her until she came. I'd let her jerk me off until I blew a load all over her hand. Just the memory has me glancing down at her hair tie around my wrist.

*Deep breath.*

*Inhale.*

*Exhale.*

*Make her proud.*

I move to hover over Allisandra, the knife firmly gripped in my right hand as I gently begin to trail it over her neck. I could jab it into her jugular and spare her the pain of what's going to happen, but I won't.

What I feel broken inside of me is immeasurable; someone else should come close to feeling it too.

I place the blade between my teeth, holding it firmly in place as I slip a hand between her legs.

She's already wet.

It makes me chuckle even though it shouldn't.

Leaning my face a little closer to hers, I slip my middle finger into her cunt and she lets out a strangled sound. I can't tell if she's enjoying it, terrified, or maybe both.

"Hold your hand up, kid," Lakyn suddenly says, his voice ripe with interest.

I pull my hand away from her fuck hole and show him. My middle finger glistens in the dim light of the room and he nods in appreciation. "Keep going."

My attention immediately goes back to Allisandra as I resume fingerfucking her. I can feel the subtle rocking of her hips as tears stream down her cheeks. Her eyes are closed tightly, and it brings a smile to my face as I take the knife from my teeth.

"Hey," I whisper to her softly.

When she doesn't open her eyes again, I push my forefinger into her and stretch her hole further.

"Want another one or are you going to look at me?" I ask her in a quiet tone. Her eyes fly open as our eyes lock and I tilt my head to the side. "Does it hurt?"

She nods rapidly but she's lying.

I haven't even begun to hurt her yet and she knows it.

"Liar," I whisper as I lean down and press my lips lightly against her neck. Another finger into her cunt to stretch it out even further and she grunts in pain. But it's not enough for my liking. She's nowhere near close to feeling the pain that I do, so I slip another finger into her. Forcing all four in makes her instantly clench her core and I smirk.

"Open up or I'll have to cut it open," I threaten in a soft tone, tapping her thigh with the blade.

Another strangled noise, another stream of tears down her cheeks, but that only gets me harder.

Instead of giving her a little bit of mercy and pulling my fingers out, I manage to cram my thumb in and shove forward. She screams through the gag, and it's like an electric current buzzing over my skin. It takes some effort, but when my hand is fully encased inside of her walls, I make a fist.

"Well shit," Lakyn remarks as I use my fist to assault her pussy. I don't start slowly, I'm uncaring in my movements, and the harder and deeper I try to push, the wider her eyes get. I tuck the knife back in my teeth so I can brace my hand on the bed for leverage.

Another loud sob escapes her as she clenches her walls, pushing as hard as she can in an attempt to expel my fist.

And I finally give her the reprieve she's so desperately seeking because my dick is hard as fuck and ready to take over.

Lakyn lets out a low whistle when he sees my fist is slick with her juices and a streak of blood. It seems that I may have torn her, but I was so wrapped up in making her feel the pain instead of the pleasure that I didn't realize it. And if I had, I wouldn't have given a shit.

I remove the knife from my teeth as I wipe my fist on the sheets, then reach down and cut her ankles free. With three killers in the room, there's no way in hell she'll make a run for it.

I move quickly, pushing her legs apart, then sit up so I can slide my boxers off. After I've tossed them over the side of the bed, I turn my attention fully back on the little Satanist that could.

"No way am I sitting this one out," Lakyn suddenly says. I glance over at him and as he begins to undress, I roll my eyes.

I won't protest, though.

If he's busy fucking this waste, then it'll be easy enough to stick him while he's distracted.

Lakyn gives his dick a couple of tugs as he climbs onto the bed and kneels next to Allisandra's head.

"I'm gonna take that out of your mouth so you can gag on something else. If you bite me, I'll rip your throat out with my fucking teeth. Got it?" he warns her with a malicious grin on his face.

*He looks like a devil when he smiles like that.*

When she nods, he sticks his fingers into the gag, shoving it further down her throat before he pulls it out and flings it over his shoulder.

"Gotta make sure that throat is nice and ready for me," he tells her with a smirk. Turning his attention to me, his eyes harden, "Get to work."

I do as I'm told and push my dick into her. She groans as her ass lifts slightly off the bed. That's when Lakyn grabs her by the back of the head and shoves his cock roughly down her throat. He begins to piston his hips, placing a hand on the headboard to balance himself. I watch for a moment as Lakyn grunts with each thrust, and only look away when he reaches over and slaps me on the top of the head.

"Didn't I tell you to get to work?" he snaps at me through bated breaths.

*If he hits me one more goddamn time, I'm going to fucking kill him.*

With the knife in my hand, I begin to move my hips. I push hard, fast, and deep, feeling like I'm locked into a competition with Lakyn who seems damn determined to break her fucking neck with the way he's fucking her mouth.

I grunt as I bring the knife up and rip her shirt open. A sliver of blood appears almost instantly on her tits. I lean down and lick it away, before I begin to suckle on her nipple. Biting, grinding it between my teeth, then bring the knife up and cut her again.

She lets out a pained sound but it's still not enough for me. I don't *feel* her pain and that's the only way she can get me to stop.

"Fuck off," Lakyn suddenly barks, followed by the sound of a body crashing into the table. I open my eyes and glance over, finding Daphne through the haze and smirk when I realize that she's tried to join in and he rebuffed her.

Again.

"Back up," Lakyn says to me as he finally pulls his dick out of Allisandra's throat. When I don't move fast enough, he makes a move to hit me again, but I dodge his hand and pull out of her.

"Stop putting your goddamn hands on me," I growl at him and he laughs as he pushes Allisandra up to a seated position as he sits down on the bed.

"Maybe you're mine after all," he declares wryly. "Now, let me show you something." He smacks her hips and she pitches forward, falling against me, body trembling with how hard she's crying, but I hold her at arm's length. Lakyn spits into the palm of his hand and palms his dick, giving himself a few good strokes, before he nods at me to push her back.

"This"—he begins as he pulls her roughly onto his lap—"happens to be my favorite hole. Because it's so…" He slips Allisandra onto his lap, the head of his dick pressed against her asshole. "Fucking tight." After his little gem of wisdom has finished, he reaches up and grabs her by the shoulders, forcing her onto him.

She gags almost instantly from the pain, letting out a weak cry through clenched teeth, and I run my hands back through my sweaty hair. Lakyn lets out his breath in a woosh as he shimmies a little and gets comfortable against the headboard.

"Alright, now stick your dick into her other hole and let's get his party started," he orders, snapping his fingers at me.

I hesitate for a moment, but when his normally bright blue eyes become almost black, I know this isn't up for debate. Taking a deep breath, I scoot up the bed, grip her legs, and shove my dick into her.

We're beyond being gentle and besides, no one was gentle with Wills, so why should I be now?

"Come on girl, impress us," Lakyn hisses into her ear as I start pushing into her. It takes him no time to start thrusting upwards, and as Allisandra's face turns crimson from the assault, a tear rolls down my cheek.

Only this time, it's not for Willa.

It's for me.

I'm becoming the very fucking monster I've come to know and hate because somewhere deep down inside… I still want him to accept me and love me as his own.

"Please," she whines quietly, but I know she's not talking to us. She knows we're not going to stop. Maybe she's talking to Satan, but I don't think he's going to save her. No one is.

Closing my eyes, I grit my teeth as I fuck her harder, deeper, resting my forehead against hers when I feel her rip slightly. By the time we're done with her she's going to have one hole instead of two, but it doesn't matter.

Nothing does.

*Except for Willa.*

Lakyn surprises me with strength I didn't even know he had when he shoves her forward and I end up on my back with Allisandra on top of me. He grips her by the hips as he slips his dick back into her and begins to fuck her so violently that the bed begins to shake.

I reach down and force my dick back into her when the opportunity presents itself. It was a hit or miss with the way he's trying to fuck her through the bed, and me along with her, but he finishes faster than I thought he would.

He leans his head back and lets out a loud, annoying moan before he chuckles, smacks her ass, and pulls out of her.

"Gee, thought you'd be better than that, Pops," I say, taking a swipe at him, but he brushes it off as he goes back to the chair and sits down. Casting a glance at Daphne who's perched on the table again watching him with her adoring, groupie eyes, he sucks his teeth and shakes his head.

"Ever fucked someone in the ass?" he asks as he pulls a cigarette out of his pack of smokes. "It's like a vacuum. Sucks the dick right in and hugs it the entire time."

I'm almost unaware of Allisandra on top of me until she whimpers. I shove her off and sit up, moving the knife from one hand to the other, thoughts of revenge swelling inside me.

"You'd have to be a lot faster than I am," Lakyn tells me with a pleasant smile. He blows out a ring of smoke before resting his elbow on the table and rubbing the side of his face with his thumb. "Think you can make a move I won't be able to stop? Try me, little boy. I'm getting bored again as it is."

I turn my face away for a moment before I shake my head and he chuckles.

"Didn't think so. Now finish your meal then clean this shit up. I'm gonna take a shower and when I get back out here, I expect to have a nice, tidy spot to sleep on. Oh, and you two get the floor."

Lakyn stubs his cigarette out in the plastic ashtray that sits in the middle of the table, then picks up one of the bags that Daphne brought in, ruffles my hair on the way by, then slams the bathroom door shut.

And now I'm left with a choice.

Let Allisandra go and kill Daphne.

Or kill them both.

## SIXTEEN

## No More Pretending

DAPHNE

I'm turned on and frustrated that I didn't get to play with them. The bitch on the bed is just lying there, limp and pathetic, and I don't understand why she doesn't see how lucky she is. So many people go their entire lives without ever meeting anyone worth the oxygen they use—and Lakyn actually fucked her.

*But he pushed me away.*

I rub at the spot on my ribs where I know I earned a bruise by falling into the table, but it's my own fault. I shouldn't have interfered with his attempt to bond with Aftyn.

Not like Aftyn is actually putting any effort in. He just sits there and watches Lakyn walk into the bathroom then stares at the door while the girl whimpers.

"Going to make Daddy proud?" I ask and his head whips around to glare at me. Turning on my sweetest smile, I lean back on the table and swing my legs back and forth. "What's the problem, pretty boy? Can't finish without him?"

"Fuck off," he snarls and grabs the priestess by the throat, yanking her back to the middle of the bed. When he shoves her legs apart, I get a look at the mess between her thighs and I don't think she'll be too upset when they finally decide to kill her. Aftyn keeps his hand wrapped tight around her neck as he shoves his dick inside her again. She sputters, trying to twist under him to get her hands free, but I watched Lakyn tie her up and I know she's not going anywhere.

The bed is cheap, old, and the headboard smacks against the wall as the mattress springs creak in time with every rough thrust. Aftyn has a nice body, and I don't mind watching him, but he keeps crying. I can see the shine on his cheeks where he's tried to wipe them away, but it just proves how pathetic he is. I'm sure he's next on Lakyn's list. Maybe after we meet this Beatrix chick that Lakyn is so fixated on.

"You're nothing, you're fucking nothing," Aftyn growls just before he thrusts hard and stills, a low groan rolling out of him as he comes deep inside her while the muscles on his back twitch.

*Apparently he can finish something after all.*

I hop off the table and grab my backpack, dropping it in the chair to dig out one of my knives. I've got so many pretty ones, each with their own little memory connected to them, but I need to choose one quickly because I know I'm going to have to finish off the Satanic bitch since—

A choked cry yanks my attention, and I'm mesmerized by the sight of Aftyn plunging the knife into the girl's chest over and over. He's still got her pinned under him, dick buried to the hilt, hand on her throat to keep her quiet, and I can't move at all for a moment. It's vicious and raw, and I sit back on the edge of the table just to enjoy the show. *This* is who Aftyn is under the mask, and I don't know why he clings to the fiction of who he tried to be for Willa when he could be this free all the time.

When he sits up, breathing hard, he releases her throat but there's no breath left in that corpse to make a noise anyway. She's painted in brilliant slashes of red, a deeper crimson pooling on her stomach, and I give in to the temptation to step closer for a better look. Aftyn's staring down at her, and I wonder what he's thinking.

Is this his first time letting that side out?

Did I get to see him pop that cherry?

Tilting my head I let my gaze slide down his blood-spattered abs, and I'm distracted by the way his dick slides out of her so I don't catch the fact that he's brought the knife back up until he plunges it into her stomach and drags it down.

*Dumbass.* I wrinkle my nose, knowing how bad she's going to stink, and we can't just toss her out the door. Plus, she's already soaking the bed. "This isn't exactly nice and tidy."

"You bitch..." he growls, and I just smile at him when he turns that feral expression on me. His eyes are empty right now, pretty blue voids just like his daddy's, and with all that blood dripping down his skin, I've never been more attracted to him. I've always liked seeing who people really are, deep down under all the masks they wear, and I think that's why I don't react fast enough when he lunges at me.

"Shit!" A searing pain flashes on my thigh as I stumble back and hit the floor hard. The second I try to push myself away from him, I realize my right leg fucking *hurts*, but I barely get a peek at the blood soaking my jeans before he's off the bed and coming for me with the knife in his hand.

"I'm gonna fucking kill you for what you did to Wills." Aftyn's eyes are still empty, and all I can do is laugh as I lunge for my backpack and yank it off the chair. He swipes at me with the knife, but I manage to kick his arm away with my good leg. The movement still sends a burning shot of pain up my other one, but it's worth it to avoid another slash. "Why the fuck are you laughing?" he screams, and I grab the first handle I wrap my fingers around and pull it out of my bag.

Pointing the knife toward him, I force myself to my feet, stumbling back into the wall by the door when my leg doesn't want to hold me up. Giggling a little, I can tell he's trying to figure out a way past my knife, but I know how to distract him. "How does it feel, Aftyn?"

"How does what feel!" he shouts, and I can't help but laugh again as I try to stabilize myself.

"Dropping your mask. Don't you like it? How freeing it is?" I ask, smiling at him when his brow furrows, fist still white-knuckle tight around the knife's handle. "It's so much better when you stop pretending to be someone you aren't. Willa isn't here anymore. You don't have to keep—"

"Don't say her fucking name!" he roars, moving toward me again, but I wave my knife back and forth, and he stops in his tracks.

"Tut tut, Aftyn. I've gutted a lot more people than you have, but I really don't want to kill you until Lakyn is done with you."

"Fucking try it. I'll cut you open just like you did to Willa, except I won't cut your goddamn throat," he threatens, moving a half-step closer as if it's going to drive his next point home. "You're going to feel every single second of that pain, bitch. Every fucking bit of it."

"Maybe," I admit, because anything is possible, but I honestly don't think he has the balls for it. Tilting my chin toward the dead girl currently drenching the bed in her blood, I lower my knife a fraction. "But look at what you were able to do when you dropped the mask, Aftyn. *That* is the most honest I've ever seen you be." Smiling, I take a deep breath, remembering the beauty of his strikes. "It was... pure. Raw. Unrestrained. Didn't it feel good to let that part of you out to play?"

His eyes flicker to the floor, knife still pointed at me, but eventually he risks a glance at her and there's not a hint of shame or disgust on his face. If anything, I see a flicker of pride.

"That's all Lakyn is trying to do for you, Aftyn. He wants you to become who you were always meant to be. He's trying to give you the opportunity to do it, and you have no idea how lucky you are to have someone who accepts you for who you are."

"Lucky?" Aftyn repeats quietly, turning back toward me. "You think I'm *lucky*? You fucking cunt. You don't know anything about me. You don't know anything about Willa! If you hadn't blindsided her, she would've taken you down easily, but you didn't even give her a chance because you knew you'd lose."

Another giggle bubbles up, and I'm grateful for the rush of adrenaline that's turned the burning ache in my leg from an eight down to a three. Pushing out my lower lip, I give my best little girl pout, baiting him. "Wanna hurt me, Aftyn?"

He opens his mouth to say something else, but the click of the bathroom door opening draws both of our attention to Lakyn as he pauses at the door and then starts to laugh.

"God damn… looks like I missed some fun." He's beautiful as he strides across the room with a towel around his waist, glancing down at the corpse on the bed before he passes right between Aftyn and me and drops into the chair at the table to grab his smokes. Flicking the lighter, he pops a cigarette between his teeth and lights it, his eyes skimming over my leg before turning back to Aftyn and letting out a few smoke rings. "So, kid, you finally decide to drop some balls, get your dick wet in some pussy, and handle the party favor… but you fuck it up when you go after Red?" Lakyn chuckles, jerking a thumb toward me. "This little psycho just too much for you?"

"I'll kill her right now if you want me to," Aftyn snaps and all I can do is giggle. I've still got the knife in my hand and if Lakyn gives the word, I'll be more than happy to show him what's under *my* mask. Even as vicious as Aftyn was with the priestess, it's a lot different when the victim can fight back. He's grinding his teeth as he glares at me, his face flushing red, and then he shouts, "Stop fucking laughing!"

"That's enough!" A loud *pop* makes me jump when Lakyn slams his hand on the table. Rubbing at his forehead, he takes a deep breath before he points between the two of us with the cigarette in his hand. "I'm not going to listen to you two arguing or shouting anymore. I'm tired, and I already told you I wanted the bed tidy by the time I came out. So, keep your mouth shut and get to work, kid."

"I'm not your boyfriend, I don't jump when you say jump, Pops." Aftyn turns his glare on Lakyn, but the man just smirks.

Taking a long drag of smoke, he lets it out in a slow stream as his eyes trail Aftyn from top to bottom. He's still naked and covered in the priestess's blood, but Lakyn doesn't seem fazed at all as he holds his palm out toward me. "Give me the knife, Red."

I flip the short knife around and lay the handle on his open hand. It's a risk. I know Lakyn could kill me if he wanted to, but I don't think he wants to yet. Right now, Aftyn is the one pissing him off. Lakyn takes another drag on his cigarette before setting it in the ashtray and looking over the knife.

"You think I'm scared of you, old man? I'm not your bitch and I'm not going to—" Aftyn's words are cut off when Lakyn bursts out of the chair, moving so quick that I'm not completely sure how he got his hand around the back of Aftyn's neck, but I can tell by the wide-eyed look in Aftyn's eyes that the knife is somewhere he definitely doesn't want it.

"Pretty sure I told you to shut your mouth, didn't I?" Lakyn asks, flashing a grin as he shifts to the side, and I can see him tapping the flat of the blade against the underside of Aftyn's dick when he glances at me. "And, Red, didn't I tell him that he'd need to be faster than me if he wanted to make a move?"

"You did," I reply, unable to bite back the smile that spreads over my lips as Aftyn tries to look tough even though the panic is written all over his wide-eyes and tense body language.

"See? I even warned you, kid, but it looks like you're still not ready to challenge me." Lakyn's arm moves a bit and Aftyn lifts onto his toes, and I can't help but hold my breath at the possibilities. "Time to make a choice. Sure you wanna fight me, kid?"

Keeping his jaw clenched tight, Aftyn drops the knife to the floor, staring at the wall as he lifts his hands. Chuckling, Lakyn moves the blade away and smacks Aftyn upside the head hard enough to send him stumbling forward.

"That's what I thought. Clean up the fucking mess you made and put that bitch in the bathroom." Dropping back into the chair, Lakyn sets my knife next to him on the table and picks up his cigarette to pull in another lungful of smoke. "Don't even think about it, kid, or this time I'll cut your balls off so you don't try to use them again."

*Was Aftyn actually looking at the knife on the ground? Idiot.*

I have no idea how Aftyn has survived as long as he has with such poor instincts. Lakyn gave him a pass, but the second he stepped away Aftyn was eyeing the fucking blade like he stood a single chance.

*Please let me kill him, Lakyn. I promise I'll make you proud.*

"Better get a move on, kid. Time's ticking away." Lakyn grins, lounging back in the chair as Aftyn finally turns away from him.

It doesn't take long for him to yank the ruined comforter and sheets from under the mattress, tossing them over the priestess' mangled corpse, but the wad of twisted, bloody fabric is too big for him to get his arms around it.

Sighing, I test my injured leg, and it seems to be able to hold my weight now, even though it hurts like a bitch. I'll get my chance to kill Aftyn eventually, or I'll get to watch Lakyn do it, and honestly I don't care much which direction things go—I just plan on being the last one standing when Lakyn Meyer is done with this reunion trip. Until then, I slap the sweet smile back on my face and limp over to the bed, grabbing the end of the pile that holds her legs. "Get the other end. I'll help."

"I don't need your fucking help." Aftyn doesn't even look at me as he sniffles, swiping under his nose. He's crying, and he's not hiding it well. When he finally manages to get his arms around the other end where her torso is hidden in layers of cheap cotton, it's clear he can't manage it by himself. He's just being an idiot. *Again.*

"Fine. Pretend I'm not helping you. I'm helping Lakyn." Picking up my end of the dead girl burrito, I swallow the groan of pain from the added weight on my leg, figuring out how to balance the awkward shape of it before I look up at him. "Well?"

After a silent glare in my direction, Aftyn finally starts moving. It's clumsy, and I almost fall, but we manage to get her crammed into the corner of the bathroom.

"Move." He shoulders past me and takes the few steps to the shower without another word.

When I catch him swiping at his eyes and nose, followed by another sniff, I roll my eyes. "You're welcome, by the way."

Aftyn answers with a middle finger, but I expected nothing less. He's predictable, boring, and even when he managed to take his mask off for a minute, he couldn't handle being that real for very long. Back to hiding behind his awkward obsession with the dead girl that never gave it up for him.

I head into the room and see the blob-like stain toward the end of the mattress. While the comforter was able to absorb quite a bit of the blood, there's no mistaking the dark stain on the cheap mattress for anything else. Popping open the closet door, I lean up on my tiptoes and find what I hoped was there. An extra pillow and two blankets. Limping over to the door, I drop the pillow and blanket on the spot I've claimed for myself, and then shake the other blanket out and lay it across the bed.

"What the fuck are you doing?" Lakyn asks, sending a plume of smoke my direction.

"It's so you don't have to sleep on the mattress." I have the strangest urge to giggle when he looks me up and down, but I manage to bite my lip and drop my eyes. The sound of him sucking his teeth fills the silence for a second before he stands up and my gaze snaps back to him.

"You're not sleeping on the bed, Red."

"I know." Pointing at the pile by the door, I shrug a bit. "I've got my spot picked out."

"Good." Scooping up his cigarettes, my knife, the ashtray, and the lighter, he takes off the towel and tosses it on the chair. *Fuck.* He's beautiful. It's not just his eyes, or his face, or even his body... it's how unapologetic he is about his existence. Lakyn Meyer doesn't give a shit what anyone thinks of him, and he never tries to be average like Aftyn does. He doesn't try to be 'normal' because he never could be. He's too real, too wild, and he burns too bright for anyone to ever mistake him for boring.

I know I'm staring when he lays out on the bed—on the blanket *I* put down for him—and I keep staring as his muscles shift when he reaches over to stack his things on the bedside table and flick the light off. The room plummets into darkness, but the vision of Lakyn is still hovering behind my eyes like one of those afterburns from a bright flash.

"Hey Red?" His voice comes out of the darkness and I can feel some kind of energy running over my skin.

"Yeah?"

"If you touch me or get on the bed while I'm asleep, I'll kill you." It's not a threat it's a promise, and I know that, but I wouldn't break his rules. I want to learn from him, to show him that I can fit in his life so much better than the walking sperm donation he left behind. I hear a rustle and then the flick of a lighter and the flame lights up his face in the black, which is growing less dark as my eyes adjust to the light leaking around the door from the bathroom and the curtains on the window. Lakyn inhales and the flame disappears, followed swiftly by the smell of cigarette smoke. "Make sure the kid doesn't wake me up."

"Okay, Lakyn." I don't know how long I stand there listening to him inhale and exhale, breathing in the smoke, but eventually I hear him stub out the cigarette and roll over, the mattress creaking as he shifts, until silence settles again. The shower cut off a few minutes ago, but Aftyn is still sulking in the bathroom, and I'm frustrated because I need to look at my leg before I can go to sleep.

Eventually, my eyes adjust enough to find the shadow of the table and my backpack on the floor, and I grab it, putting it back on the chair to dig around by memory for clean clothes to change into. When the bathroom door opens a minute or two later, yellow light floods across the room, and I wave at Aftyn, whispering, "Close it!"

"Fuck off." Aftyn leaves the door open, and I sigh. Fortunately, the angle of the doorway is keeping the light off Lakyn's face, but the extra light does show me something I hadn't noticed before. Lakyn's shirt is on the floor near the bedside table, and I limp over to grab it, shoving it into my backpack before I head to the bathroom. Aftyn's propped himself in the corner of the room with the towel still wrapped around his waist, but when he notices me looking, he flips me off again, hissing out another pathetic threat. "Stay the hell way from me, because I promise, the next time I cut you, you won't be walking away from it."

"Sure thing, Aftyn. I guess you finished crying in the shower?" I ask quietly, flashing a smile at his enraged glare before I step into the bathroom and close the door behind me.

Getting the jeans down my legs is a lesson in pain management, but I bite down on my shirt to keep the groans in until I'm finally free of them.

*Fucking pussy.*

Aftyn had taken an opportunistic swipe, and if I hadn't been so impressed by what he'd done to the priestess, I would have realized he was going to come at me. But nothing teaches lessons like pain, and although the cut is deeper than I'd like, I know if I can manage to keep it pretty clean, I'll be okay. What's more important is stopping the slow leak of blood rolling down my thigh with every beat of my heart.

Living the way I have means Aftyn isn't the first asshole who's taken the opportunity to hurt me, the difference between the two of us is that I *always* come out on top. It's obvious by the car he and Willa were driving that he isn't used to life being difficult. It's why he's still moping over his not-girlfriend being dead. I doubt he's ever been on the receiving end of something like what he did to the priestess, and when he was naked, I didn't see any scars to tell a story similar to mine. People like Aftyn need others because they've never learned to function on their own.

I've never needed anyone.

I haven't even *wanted* anyone before… but I do want Lakyn. And I don't care what that means.

If he wants me in his bed, I'll be there. If he wants me on the floor, I'll sleep there. If he wants me to kill, I will.

As long as I can be around him, life will be more tolerable, and as soon as Aftyn is gone everything will be better. No more masks, no more pretending, no more waiting to see if the next car that picks me up will want to hurt me or fuck me just because I wanted a ride. No more putting up with it until they drop their guard enough for me to slit their throats and move on.

It's thinking of how different life could be with Lakyn Meyer that drags my attention to my backpack again and I pull out Lakyn's shirt, pressing it to my nose to inhale deeply. The shirt smells like him, a mixture of cigarette smoke and warm male skin—but not like the greasy bastards that pick me up all the time. No, Lakyn smells like… Lakyn. Unique and *good*.

Pulling out one of my sharper knives from its zippered pocket, I slice his shirt into long strips, and then I take my shirt off to force enough of it into my mouth to help keep me quiet—and keep me from biting my tongue—because this is going to hurt.

I take a deep breath and lay the last clean washcloth over the cut, and then wrap the first strip of his shirt around my thigh, knotting it tight to hold the cloth in place and keep pressure on it. The pain is nauseating, but I've had worse, and with Lakyn's scent against my skin I'll always have him with me. That's what gets me through the rest of the strips, even when I have to lean against the tub to keep from getting sick.

When I finally finish, the bandaging job doesn't look half bad, and with the pressure on the wound it doesn't hurt as much to move my leg.

*Or I'm just blocking out the pain, but who the fuck cares?*

Gathering the remnants of Lakyn's shirt, I know I need to hide them, because I don't think either of them would understand. It's as I'm gathering the last scraps that I realize I'm staring at the pile of bedding that holds a corpse we'll have to get rid of tomorrow. The priestess hadn't been very appreciative of the attention Lakyn showed her, not even when he complimented how good her ass had felt.

"Perfect," I whisper to myself.

When I shuffle across the bathroom floor to unwrap her, I try to ignore just how dizzy I feel so I can finish this before I go to sleep. As soon as she's revealed, I use the pile of fabric to flip her onto her ruined stomach and slide my knife into her asshole, imagining how it had been for Lakyn.

It's always amazed me how easily sharp knives can cut through skin, but I imagine it wouldn't be *this* easy if she were alive. Still, I manage to widen the hole enough to stuff the scraps of Lakyn's shirt inside her where I know his cum is already waiting. It's messy, and I get blood all over my hands, but it's… fitting. She wasn't grateful for what he'd given her, and now he'll be inside her forever.

I think even Lakyn would appreciate it—if I told him, which I won't.

I wrap her back up and scrub myself clean with the soap, dry off, then brush my teeth and hair. I have to bite down on my shirt again to get my leg into the soft, black pants that will hide the blood if it leaks through, and by the time I'm actually dressed again, I feel dead on my feet.

Blood loss and pain will do that, though.

With one last glance over the bathroom, I pack everything away and turn off the light before I open the door, staying quiet as I creep into my corner. Laying down, I face the wall and hug my backpack to my chest, giving into the exhaustion so that I can be ready for whatever Aftyn wants to throw at me next.

I'll take it, and I'll survive it, like I always do, because I'm not going back to how things were before.

I won't go back to wearing a mask all the time. No. I want to be as free as Lakyn.

## SEVENTEEN

## Snakes in the Desert

LAKYN

I grunt and smack my lips together when I wake up. I think I slept wrong because my neck feels a little hinky, but that's nothing that Red probably wouldn't throw herself off a cliff at the chance to rub out for me.

*Speaking of Red…*

I prop myself up on my elbows and glance down at my dick, smirking when I see it's just as dry as I left it.

I've met and fucked a lot of chicks in my day, though I've never met one as desperate for my dick as her.

*At least she listens when spoken to,* I think with a shrug as I sit up and rub my eyes. Glancing over into the corner of the room, I can see the kid is still asleep and I can't help but laugh at the expression on his face.

This is the first time I can honestly say that I've seen someone rage sleep before.

Red on the other hand is still on the floor, tucked neatly in a little ball, and if this were a different time and place, she would've been fucked through the wall behind her.

But she has to learn.

I don't like accepting what's thrown at me so easily.

If I get hungry enough for her, I'll wear her down, then fucking take it when I want.

Maybe I'll even let the kid have some. He seems to do better when he shoves his dick into some pussy.

I reach up and rub my neck, tilting my head to the left, then gingerly to the right.

Once I've decided that this is as good as it's going to get, I clear my throat and clap my hands together loudly.

Red springs up like she had never been asleep, wincing slightly, and the kid lets out a gasp and I laugh as his entire body starts to shake.

"What the fuck?" he grumbles as he uses the back of his hand to rub his eyes and I arch an eyebrow.

"What the fuck do you think?" I ask him with a shake of my head. "It's time to go."

"Good morning, Lakyn," Red pipes up in a groggy tone and I cut my eyes toward her. Something has to give with this one. I don't mind the worship since it's rightfully deserved, but she's taking it too fucking far even for me.

"Yeah," I say rolling my eyes as I get to my feet. I glance over at her still on the floor and have to suppress an annoyed shudder. "Someone go grab the bitch from the bathroom. We're gonna have to take her with us until we have somewhere to ditch her."

Red gets up faster than the kid, though at this point I doubt it's even a competition. She just sees it as one and that can come in handy later on down the line.

I walk over to where he's still sitting on the floor and snap my fingers in front of his face.

"You gonna let her do all of the work by herself?"

"Why not?" he shoots back. "She seems to enjoy being your goddamn lapdog. May as well let her."

"Heh."

I shrug as I go back to where I left my clothes and begin to get dressed when I realize that my shirt is missing. Turning on my heel, I glance around on the floor arch my eyebrows wondering where the fuck it could have gone.

"Hand it over," I say to her in a stern tone. It wouldn't surprise me if she tried to fuck herself with it while I was asleep.

"Hand what over?" Red asks innocently.

I return the glance with a level stare and remember that she may be useful later on. "My shirt."

She begins to chew her lower lip nervously as she moves away me and disappears into the bathroom to grab the dead chick.

Running a hand back through my hair, I turn my eyes toward the kid. He's got his back to me as he pulls on his jeans and that's when I get a great idea. When I see him attempting to pull his shirt over his head, it gives me an idea and I walk over to him and take it out of his hand.

"Thanks for the shirt," I tell him with a smirk. And when he scowls, my smirk turns into a grin.

I'll turn him into a real Meyer before this is over. Whether he likes it or not.

Red comes back into the room, dragging the wad of bedding around the dead girl, grunting like a stuck pig when I notice that she's limping.

"What happened there?" I ask with a grin.

She lowers her eyes but doesn't respond right away. Not with words, anyway.

Instead, she drops the dead chick on the carpet, scoots toward the bed and lifts her leg, planting her heel on the bed. When she pulls up her yoga pants to show me, my dick twitches at how flexible she is—but I manage to keep it down by looking at the kid and remembering that one fuck up is more than enough.

---

I TURN the dial up on the radio and begin to drum my fingers against the steering wheel in time with the piano music that floats through the speakers.

*"Just a small town girl—"*

The kid reaches over and jabs the power button almost instantly and I laugh. He's lucky that I let him sit in front with me again after being such a pussy on the way to the dump we just left, but I'd rather his company than Red's for the time being.

"Wanna know something?" I ask, glancing at him for a moment. When he turns his eyes toward me in that bitchy little way he thinks will scare me, I smile. "This shirt smells like blonde whore. You sure you never fucked that girl?"

The look on his face goes from bitchy to shocked to angry.

"Whoa!"

He reaches over and pulls on the steering wheel with all of his strength and we go careening off the side of the road. I smack his hands and when he doesn't let go, I land an elbow into the side of his head, knocking him back against his door as I spin the wheel trying to regain control of the truck.

Once I've got it under control and we're back on the road, I run a hand back through my hair.

"You're such a pussy. You'd never last a day with me at home, you know," I tell him as I glance into the rear-view mirror. Red looks completely undisturbed as she keeps her eyes on the world outside of her window. "I mean, you haven't even been able to rattle *her*, what the fuck makes you think you can get to me?"

"I wasn't trying to rattle you," he replies through clenched teeth, the pain obvious in his tone.

"Oh? Then what was that?" I ask as I reach up into the visor for the pack of smokes.

He lets out a loud sigh as he rubs the side of his head and continues to nurse the bruise that I'm sure will grow into a nice little egg in no time. "Nothing. Forget it."

"I can't. You're still here," I reply thoughtfully. "But you know what? I'm gonna keep my hands to myself for the rest of this trip. Trixie doesn't like seeing her charity cases beat to shit and I'm sure you'll become one of hers in no time."

*Actually, that's not a bad idea.*

He doesn't answer me, so I cast a casual glance in his direction then shake my head as I turn my eyes back toward the road.

"Hey, Red? How's Satan's failed superstar holding up?" I ask, looking in the rear-view mirror again.

"Fine," she replies immediately as she raises her eyes to meet mine. "She doesn't smell too bad or anything."

"She won't for a few days," I say thoughtfully. "But thankfully, she won't be with us that long. Not that this trip should be longer than a few more hours. I hope anyway."

Another hour into the drive and I'm getting antsy. Had this been twenty or so years ago, I could have pulled over and gotten my dick sucked.

*Or at the very least violated Ichabod. I wonder what he's up to.*

I blink rapidly a few times then run a hand over my face. Why the hell he's even entered my mind is beyond me, but I know that if I don't come back with his beloved 'Bea' he's going to make my life a living hell.

Although it also makes me wonder if the bullshit the kid was trying to sell me when we left my place is true.

Did he email him?

Does he have a phone I don't know about?

There are too many lingering questions that I don't have answers for and that's starting to piss me off the longer I let it settle.

I can't fully blame Ichabod for his heroic bullshit, though. Not that bringing this fucking shit show to my doorstep was heroic, but he's always wanted to make everyone around him happy no matter how they've treated him.

And that's why I'm still aggravated that he's got a hard-on for Trixie. She pretended to be his friend, pretended that she cared about him, then dumped him on me the moment the chance presented itself.

Should I be mad at her about it?

I don't know.

At the very least, I hope she has something nice to say about him when I finally talk to her because it'll do him wonders to know she still 'loves' him.

*Fucking bitch,* I think gritting my teeth.

If it wasn't for her none of this would have ever happened.

I wouldn't have had the chance to fuck in Vegas. Ichabod never would have gotten hooked on drugs and I never would have sold whatever soul she thinks I have to her in exchange for whatever the fuck it was she was trying to achieve.

"Kid?" I say to him in a quiet tone.

He turns his eyes toward me, and I can see the venom swelling up inside of him already. He's waiting for me to berate him, take another swipe at his blonde bitch friend, or maybe even reach over and smack him again, but…

I take a deep breath and let it out as I go back to focusing on the road in front of me.

"Never mind."

---

I'M STARTING to get tired again. My eyes are dry because of all of the fucking smoke that's been blowing back into my face and I need to stop to reset my batteries.

"Where are we?" the kid asks in a thick tone as he sits up, places his palms against the dashboard and stretches.

"Fuck if I know," I reply truthfully. "Maybe we should have kept the wannabe alive a little longer," I tell him with a grin.

He rolls his eyes as he crosses his arms over his chest and glances out the windshield.

"We're in the desert already?"

"Mhm," I reply as I rub my eyes again. "Once I know where I'm going, I like to get there as quickly as possible."

"So, if you know where we're going, then where are we?"

"The desert," I reply dryly. "Just sit back and shut up. You're starting to get on my nerves."

With a grunt, the kid leans his head against the window.

Another twenty minutes of driving around backroads through the Mojave Desert and I'm ready to crash the fucking truck. Thankfully there aren't any cacti close to the road.

I pull over and cut the engine, then retrieve the keys. Hopping out and stretching my legs I wander around the front of the truck. Leaning my head back, I clasp my hands and bring them over my head, feeling every muscle in my back rippling from exhaustion.

I rub the back of my neck when I'm done and glance around. I don't see whatever bullshit community Trixie's joined, but I can feel the nervous energy that turns into blind rage whenever she's around, so I know at the very least we're heading in the right direction.

Of course, had I brought Ichabod like he asked me to, he would have sniffed her cunt out a mile away.

Not that they ever fucked.

At least not to my knowledge.

I'm pretty sure that she doesn't fuck her charity cases, just lulls them into a sense of false stability then attacks like the snake that she is.

I rest against the truck, bend forward, and place my hands on my knees.

There's no time for a quick beauty nap before I see Trixie again.

When a snake is ready to strike, the only way to get it to see reason is to cut its fucking head off and that's just what I intend to do.

I just have to find her first.

And for that all I need to do is get back in the truck and follow the smoke signals.

## EIGHTEEN

## Rise of the Jackal pt. 2

AFTYN

We've been weaving around narrow roads off the highway for a while now, and the urge to jerk the wheel and send us careening into the desert is returning with a vengeance.

Lakyn Meyer is a fucking stain on this planet, and all I want to do is erase him from it. Sending the bitch in the backseat along with him is almost too kind, because I know she'd want to be with him anyway— but she deserves to die for killing Willa.

They both do.

Wrecking the truck in the middle of this wasteland won't get me anywhere though. With my luck, I'd be the only one injured and Lakyn would walk off into the sunset with this Beatrix chick while Daphne followed at his heels like the bitch she is. *Fuck that.*

I take out my pack of smokes and light one up, taking a long inhale before I crack the window and let it stream out as I exhale. I glance over at Lakyn to find him sitting in a mirror-image of me. One elbow propped on the door, cigarette in hand. The only difference is his hand is on the wheel and mine is on my knee.

*Dammit.*

I shift position and take another drag before I ask, "How do you even know this Trixie chick is even out here?"

"She is," Lakyn answers, a plume of smoke sliding out the side of his mouth.

"Because that priestess bitch said so?" I laugh and shake my head. "Right."

"Those Lucifer loving psychos are still obsessed with her, and this is where they said she'd be." Lakyn flashes a grin at me. "And you saw the way that chick looked at me. She wanted me to join their little church almost as much as she wanted my dick." He shrugs and flicks his cigarette out the window. "She told the truth. Just gotta find this place she's holed up."

"You've been driving around for hours, and the priestess said it was 'just off route 66.'" I wave my hand at the windshield that shows endless fucking desert. "We're pretty far off the highway now and there's jack-shit."

"I did expect there to be smoke signals or something," Lakyn replies, laughing as he leans forward to look up at the sky. "Doesn't it seem like there should be smoke signals coming from a place out here?"

"Just admit that you're lost, Pops."

"I'm not lost." Lakyn suddenly slams on the brakes, and the tires squeal as I barely catch myself on the dash and Daphne lets out a yelp from the backseat. His laughter only gets louder as he points out the side of the truck. "You seeing this shit?"

"Seeing what?" I snap, trying not to look as rattled as I am, but I follow his finger out the window where there's a cactus near the road decorated with sparkling gems and faded, colorful ribbons. "What the fuck is that?"

"A sign." Accelerating again, Lakyn keeps the truck at a moderate speed, eyes scanning the side of the road as more and more decorated cacti spring up, along with a handful of wooden boards with spray painted arrows on them. "Keep an eye out for smoke signals, kid. We're getting close to finding Auntie Trixie."

Rolling my eyes, I let my mind wander, daydreaming about driving the knife I've tucked away in the floorboard into Lakyn's throat. I can picture the spray of blood, the way it would look bright red with the sunlight behind it on the glass. We'd crash, but I'd be ready, and Daphne would probably be too distracted by her obsession choking on his own blood to brace for the crash. Then I'd just have to take her out, and I could wander into whatever fucking commune is out here and get a ride back into actual civilization.

"There!" Lakyn shouts, another round of laughter making my head pound as he slows the car down and turns onto a small dirt track that wouldn't look like anything at all if it weren't surrounded by cacti absolutely covered in sparkling prisms, colorful streamers, and Christmas tinsel. Stopping the car just inside the dirt 'road,' Lakyn looks around, shaking his head. "Are you fucking kidding me?"

"You found it!" Daphne pipes up from the back, and I have to grit my teeth to keep from leaning into the backseat to punch her again.

"Maybe," I grumble. Glancing out the window, I see another wooden sign tethered to a dilapidated fence and flick the last of my cigarette at it. "It may not be Trixie, but apparently there's *something* out here. This sign over here says 'Daughter of Greater Light, 1 mile,' and there's an arrow pointing that way." I point out the windshield, and Lakyn cranes his neck to look past me.

"Of course Trixie found another cult to join. So fucking predictable…" Lakyn mumbles to himself as he lets off the brake and we start bouncing over the rough excuse for a road.

Even at a crawl, Willa's SUV feels like it's about to break an axle, but eventually I can see cars and travel trailers in the distance. As we get closer, I feel Daphne grab onto the back of my seat, but it only takes one sneer for her to back off, positioning herself between the front seats so she can see.

"All these people live out here in the middle of nowhere?" Daphne asks, but neither of us even glance at her. I'm distracted by the way the light is glinting off a huge greenhouse, and the large number of people pouring out of tents and a few shitty looking buildings that look like they were constructed from mud bricks.

"What a joke," Lakyn mutters, tilting his chin toward a large sign on the left side of the road.

'*Welcome to the Daughter of Greater Light,*' it reads in big, colorful letters, and painted underneath it in smaller letters is, '*Love Lives Here.*'

"Wow." It's the only word I can think of, because nothing about this weird hippie commune seems like a place the Beatrix from Lakyn's stories would hang out. How could someone go from Lucifer-worshipping friend of the fucked-up monster next to me... to here? It has to be a mistake. After all, the priestess never actually gave a name for wherever Beatrix ended up, and just because we found some sparkly cacti in the middle of nowhere doesn't mean we're in the right place.

Of course, any place would be better than spending a single minute more around Lakyn or the redheaded cunt in the backseat. *This* fucking mess might be more than I can tolerate though. It reminds me of all those pics I've seen from the seventies where hippies braided each other's hair and talked about peace and love like the world would actually change if they just believed in it hard enough.

Idiots.

The world doesn't want peace. It just wants to destroy everyone slowly and methodically until the day we finally die.

"Welcome!" a man shouts, waving at us as Lakyn pulls the SUV off their excuse for a road and throws it into park, yanking the keys free. The man hurrying toward us has a small crowd of smiling imbeciles following him as he approaches the car. "You've found us, fellow travelers. Welcome," he repeats.

Lakyn sucks his teeth and grabs his cigarettes and the lighter before he throws the door open and climbs out, twisting his back. Willa's keys go into his pocket and I'm tempted to grab the knife in the floorboard, but I figure that wouldn't be the best introduction to these hippies, so I leave it behind and get out of the SUV with my smokes and lighter in my hand.

Daphne is already out and walking around to hover behind Lakyn, but I'm taking my time. She can continue being the eager little bitch while I figure out if I'll get the chance to slit Lakyn's throat out here and take the keys off him.

"I'm Sun Wolf, a Light Weaver here in our community, and—"

"Sun Wolf?" Lakyn repeats, a bark of laughter leaving him and continuing, but this wolf guy doesn't seem bothered at all. He's just… smiling.

"Yes. It's my Light Weaver name. If you decide to stay with us you'll choose your own name so that you can walk in the glory of The Daughter just like—"

"I really don't care," Lakyn says, cutting the asshole off as he lights a cigarette and blows the smoke toward the man's face. "I'm here for Trixie."

"Trixie?" Sun Wolf the light-whatever repeats, glancing back at the others near him as he brings his hands together. "I'm afraid I don't recognize that name, but I'll be glad to spread the word. We've had so many Children of the Light join us over the years, and it's hard to remember everyone's old names from out in the world."

"*Right.*" Lakyn sucks his teeth again, looking over the gathered people, and the Sunny Wolf idiot finally starts to look a little anxious when we stay silent.

"I apologize, it's been a few months since anyone found us. Who sent you to us?" Wolf dude asks, and Lakyn shoves a hand back through his hair, taking another drag before he looks back at him.

"Chick named Alexandra. A high priestess back in New Mexico."

"Allisandra," Daphne whispers, stepping closer to Lakyn, but it only takes a glance from him to stop her in her tracks, and I chuckle to myself at how fucking pathetic she is.

"Yeah, Allisandra. She said Trixie was out here," Lakyn adds, ashing his cigarette.

"Ah, well, I'm not familiar with her, but our family here is broad, and all that matters is you've found your way to us." Wolf guy puts his palms together and bows slightly. "How about we give you a tour of our community, and Akasha here will go speak to The Daughter. She knows all within the bounds of her kingdom here on our earthly plane. If anyone will know if your Trixie is one of us, it will be her."

"What the hell, sure. Lead the way, Wolfy," Lakyn says, chuckling as he flashes his grin at one of the women standing behind the weirdo. The bitch actually blushes and smiles back at Lakyn, and all I want to do open the back of the SUV and let Allisandra roll out so the cunt could see exactly whose attention she's seeking.

"Wonderful! Follow me," Wolf replies cheerfully, waving an arm back toward the more densely populated area of the commune. More smiling, happy people wave at us as we walk along, listening to the imbecile talk about all of the shit their community is so proud of. I'm barely paying attention to any of it as I light up a cigarette and follow a little ways behind Lakyn and Daphne.

I was right about the shiny building being a greenhouse, and he goes on and on about it and how 'overjoyed' they are to have two wells on the property, which apparently provide water for everyone there.

"We have almost two hundred members following The Light of The Daughter," some chick adds, and Wolf turns his zombie-happy smile on her.

"That's right, Raindrop. Some have come to The Light on their own, but we have families like yours as well."

"Like mine?" Lakyn almost chokes on his inhale of smoke, laughing as he jerks a thumb over his shoulder. "That little shit is supposedly my kid, but the apple fell pretty far from the badass tree—if you know what I mean." He laughs a little more as he tilts his head toward Daphne. "And Red here is just a fan."

"Oh, well, you're all welcome," Wolf replies, still smiling, and the overall vibe of this place is starting to make my skin crawl. It's like everybody volunteered for a lobotomy, and I'm just waiting for whatever crazy fuck is in charge of this shitshow to show themselves. "Raindrop, why don't you explain how we earn for the community? I'm going to help Akasha look for The Daughter so she can welcome them properly."

"Of course, Sun Wolf." The peppy little brunette that's been eye-fucking Lakyn the entire walk steps closer as we stop in front of the rough, adobe buildings. Smiling, she points off to the side where a series of tables are set up. "It's not much, but we do make our own beads here, decorating them with the colors that the Earth provides, and then we make jewelry. We also have a few carpenters who create other pieces that several of our members travel and sell to—"

"Listen, I'm not going to be here very long. I'm just here to let the kid meet his Aunt Trixie, and then I'm gone." Lakyn draws on the cigarette, and let's smoke drift from his mouth as he looks the chick up and down and adds, "You're wasting your fucking breath."

"No one is required to stay here. This is a place of love, and The Daughter helps us all to live in The Light." Raindrop shrugs a shoulder, and I can't help but wonder what she looks like under the flower skirt and loose-fitting shirt. "Once you meet her, you'll understand."

"Not fucking likely," Lakyn replies. He drops his cigarette and crushes it into the ground while he lights another one. Most of the crowd around us has wandered off, and I can see campfires getting lit around the sprawling commune, the scent of burning wood blending with the cigarette smoke on the breeze. Everyone looks vaguely dirty, like the sand and dust of the desert has coated everyone and everything with a layer of it, and it makes my skin itch.

I don't even know why I'm fucking here, other than it's the place Lakyn wanted to go, and I'm still waiting for my chance to kill the fucker. Sitting in the corner of that damn hotel room last night, in the dark, listening to Lakyn breathing, I'd fantasized about killing him. I'd even thought about how perfect it would be for his blood to join Allisandra's in the mattress... but something held me back. Every time I pictured stabbing Lakyn, I saw Allisandra instead. The way her eyes had gone wide the first time the knife went in, the way her cunt had squeezed my dick like a fist, and the gurgling sound of her breath as she died.

Killing her hadn't made me feel better. It's why I'd gone after Daphne, because I knew killing *her* would ease some of the emptiness inside me... but I'd fucked that up.

I don't know if it was all the adrenaline or the fact that I'd just come, but my reaction time wasn't fast enough and by the time I'd got off the bed and had my feet under me again, ready to kill her, she had a fucking knife in her hand. That fucking backpack of hers is apparently filled with blades, which is just one more reason why I have to catch her off guard. I want her unarmed and vulnerable, just like when she killed Willa.

I didn't give a shit about killing Allisandra. Hell, I don't know what I'd expected to feel after it. Maybe I thought I'd at least feel a little victorious… but no. I just felt emptier. Angrier.

The only deaths that will make me feel any better are Lakyn and Daphne's, and the next opportunity I get to kill them, I won't hesitate. Even if it means I go down in the process.

I'm so focused on the back of Lakyn's head that at first I don't realize the people cheering around me, but it sinks in slowly and I follow their gazes to something… something incredible. The sun is setting behind the woman walking toward us, and I swear it looks like she's glowing. Golden fire radiates around her head, her blonde hair shining where it flows over her shoulders, and as she spreads her arms wide, acknowledging the people bowing toward her, I can't tear my eyes away from the way her hips sway.

She's beyond beautiful, and while the smile on everyone else's faces have made them look like idiots, the smile on her face looks like peace. Real peace.

And she's looking right at me.

I walk toward her, ending up a little ahead of Lakyn when I stop because I'm worried if I walk too close she'll step away, and I don't want that. Her dress is tight to her body, the round of her breasts revealed by the deep plunge of the neckline that stops somewhere around her waist, and the golden bracelets around her wrists tinkle and chime as she lets her arms rest at her side.

"It's been so long," she says to me, and her voice is dream-like. Soft and warm. If *this* is The Daughter, I can see why so many people have decided to follow her, because the way she's looking at me makes me believe I might be okay as long as I'm near her.

Then Lakyn shatters the connection between us as he lets out a sharp laugh. "You've gotta be fucking kidding me."

## NINETEEN

## Cults for Dummies

LAKYN

I clear my throat and shift on my feet as I stare at the golden spikes rising from her hair like a fucked-up tiara. I don't get why Trixie is dressed up like some kind of demi-god, or why she looks so fucking happy about it, but she'll snap out of it as soon as we get to talking. She'll remember that she's the miserable bitch that I know and hate, and she'll hop in the fucking truck to go see Ichabod. Once that's done and over with, she'll be out of my fucking hair forever —and his.

"Been a long time, Trixie," I say to her in an even tone as I cross my arms over my chest and rock back and forth on my feet. But if she hears me, it's not registering. "Beatrix St. Germain," I say a little louder, feeling the agitation rising like a fury inside of me. "You there?"

Her eyes finally tear away from the kid long enough to look into mine. Her smile falters slightly as a look of confusion briefly flashes in them, then she turns her attention back to *him*. The latest bane of my fucking existence.

"I can't believe you found me," she says in her brand-new, warped tone of voice. She holds her hands out toward the kid and when he takes a step forward, I reach for the back of his shirt and yank him back where I want him.

"Stay," I tell him in a testy tone, a grin starting to slip across my lips.

"Oh, kind sir," Trixie intercedes with a brief shake of her head. "Here on the Holy Ground of Light, we don't treat each other with anything other than love."

I arch an eyebrow at her incredulously, my grin faltering as my mouth opens slightly. Trixie's never been all there, but I think wherever 'there' may have gotten lost somewhere at the start of the road behind us.

*Well, there's only one way to snap her out of this shit.*

"Ichabod misses you," I continue conversationally. When the kid snickers next to me, I give him such a withering glare that his eyes lower to his feet and he scuffs the dirt with the tip of his sneaker.

"Who? I'm sorry," Trixie replies with a kind smile. "I don't know anyone by that name."

I go rigid.

Anger begins to course through my veins as I take a step closer to her and peer into her eyes.

"Come again?"

"But you, I've missed greatly dear friend," she says reaching over to lay her hand on the kid's shoulder. "Have you been well?"

*What the fuck is happening right now?*

He nods with such vigor that it makes me want to smack the back of his head to see if I can get it to bobble even faster. Red shuffles a little closer to me and I control the urge to give her a withering stare. Apparently, that doesn't work on the holy ground of whatever, and it's frustrating me as much as it's pissing me off.

But it also gives me an idea.

"When I tell you to," I say to her out of the corner of my mouth and she looks over at me in confusion. I lean a little closer and turn on a mega-watt, charming smile. I can see the realization in her eyes of what she wants, and while I would love to do it myself, I can't go back to Ichabod with Trixie's blood on my hands.

I'd never hear the end of it.

"I've been better," the kid says, rubbing the back of his neck. A sigh escapes from Trixie as she reaches forward and wraps her arms around him. The way her chin rests on his shoulder, eyes closed, almost like she's trying to give him some kind of touchy, pick me up, has me more ready than ever to tell Red to take her fucking head off.

*Not yet.*

"When you're done feeling up my kid, let's chat," I snap in a loud tone.

"Oh, Lakyn," she murmurs as she opens her eyes and looks into the kid's face. "I'm so happy that you brought your father to us. We'll help him heal any anger he has in his heart as well."

She thinks...? She can't possibly...

"Um, Trixie?" I intercede, snapping my fingers at her to get her attention away from the kid. When she looks at me with those hazed over eyes of hers, my heart drops into my fucking stomach. "Are you... high?"

Her having her wires crossed on who's who right now doesn't fucking matter, but if she's smacked up on something, that's going to bring a shitstorm her way that even her little holy sun fuckers won't be able to protect her from.

She places a hand to her mouth as she giggles, looping an elbow with the kid's. The longer he stands next to her looking at me with that smug look on his face, the more I wonder if I should cut his goddamn head off too.

"Oh no, dear friend," she says, her body beginning to sway slightly again. She lifts a hand to the sky, and I follow briefly with my eyes, before lowering them back to her. "We don't need narcotics to embrace the way of the Light. We simply drink from the Cactus of Ambrosia and let the energies of the Earth around us take hold."

I grit my teeth.

So they don't do drugs, they make their own and drink it down. Makes perfect fucking sense.

"Listen, bitch," I bark, closing the gap between us and pointing a finger in her face. "I didn't get your fucking charity case off of drugs so you could fucking get on them."

Trixie gently moves my hand to the side as she rests her head on the kid's shoulder, the psycho-bitch smile never leaving her face.

"He has more anger than you, but don't worry. You brought him to the right place, and we'll help him as best as we can."

I run a hand over my chin and glance at Red, who's looking at me with those damn adoring eyes of hers.

It could be so easy right now to let her take down the newly crowned Queen Bitch of the Desert, but I want more answers. And I want her to fucking know who it's from.

"Let's try this again," I say through grit teeth. "*I* am Lakyn Meyer. You remember the Den back at the Light of Lucifer? Sybil? Hail Goats? The burden you fucking left on me after you killed Sergio on your little quest to become Satan's Favorite Superstar?" At this point, I'm shouting at her, my body is shaking, and I'm angrier than I've ever been in my life, but I don't know what else to do with all of the pent-up rage that's building.

"No, my child," she corrects as she reaches forward and places a hand to my cheek.

I jerk back violently. The way she kept Ichabod smacked up on that road trip, fuck knows if she's got cactus water hidden somewhere in her goddamn hand and I refuse to be one of these drugged out assholes.

"This is Lakyn," she continues as she rests her head on the kid's shoulder. "You're his father and he brought you here to bathe in the Light. There are no burdens in the desert, no death or decay. Only love."

*Fuck this.*

I snap my fingers toward Red then get ready to see the best performance of her life. I'm sure she's been aware of being in Trixie's shadow the entire way here and I bet she'd take her down with pleasure. But when nothing happens, I cross my arms over my chest again and glance over my shoulder.

"Come on Re—"

I turn around completely and narrow my eyes as I scan the newly gathered crowd in confusion. Red's nowhere to be seen. Either she slipped away to look around or one of them slipped her something and she's off joining the hippie dwellers of the desert.

"You know what's sucks?" I begin conversationally as I reach into my pocket for a smoke. I pop one between my teeth, light it, then turn to face Trixie and the kid. She's looking up at him with such affection that I'm about to blow chunks all over both of them. "You don't deserve this." When she looks over at me again, I gesture around with a hand. "Of course, you never could help but one-up me as best as you could at every turn. Cults have always been my thing, Trixie, and look at you go. Rubbing your glories in my face again."

Trixie smiles at me as she finally let's go of the kid and places both of her hands on my shoulders.

I look down into her drugged out eyes and grit my teeth again. She's gonna end up owing me a trip to the dentist by the time I get out of this goddamn place.

"Mr. Meyer, you're welcome here," she assures me with a nod. "There's no reason to harbor such anger and hatred in your heart. Lakyn brought you to me to help you. I welcome the challenge and look forward to helping you find the good inside of you."

I grab her wrist and clench my hand around it like a vise, but she doesn't even flinch. "What did I tell you about putting your fucking hands on me?" I growl at her, giving her rough shove away from me.

Her laughter sounds like a set of chimes being tickled by the wind and at this point, I'm ready to just fuck off back home since Red isn't around to split her goddamn head wide open.

She leans her body against the kids then looks up at him with a smile on her face. "He thinks that he's Lakyn. That's funny, don't you think?"

*But not before I try at least one more time.*

"You met Ichabod when he was fifteen years old. It was just before his sixteenth birthday. You were seventeen going on eighteen. I was at home far away from this bullshit, probably fucking a really fine piece of ass, but that's neither here nor there. You found him digging around in garbage to feed his junkie family and you took him to get pizza that day. Then he met you that night for a cookie or some shit and you guys celebrated his birthday. You repaid the favor by making us all celebrate your twenty-first in a goddamn van going on a magical adventure to kill Sergio—who you handed Ichabod to on a silver platter I might add—so you could ascend and be Satan's number one bitch. Any of this clicking in that muddled brain of yours?"

A sympathetic smile appears on her lips as she shakes her head. "I'm sorry but I don't know anyone named Ichabod. I've never wanted to glorify a deity and I don't recall any of this, but they sound like delusions, Mr. Meyer. If you drink from the Cact—"

"Go fuck yourself," I snarl, cutting her off as I flick my smoke at her face, then turn on my heel.

"Don't worry, Pops!" the kid calls out after me. "I'll make sure that she's taken care of!"

I choose not to listen to him because if I do, I'll fire up the truck and run them all over on my way out of here.

What fucks me off entirely is that she has no memory of Ichabod. She destroyed his life and chose to brush off remembering him so she could be glorified by a bunch of poisoned water slingers that don't know anything about her past.

None of it.

Not the way she used people. Manipulated anyone she slithered her tight little body against to get them to do her bidding. Coerced them with a silver tongue to bind themselves to her for her own goddamn wants.

All of her past is behind her and she thinks that's okay.

I guess she forgot my equation, though.

I don't like blondes.

I don't like druggies.

Trixie's crossed the line from being somewhat safe to the top of my favorite list.

I pull open the door of the truck and get in. Once I've got the keys in the ignition and the fucking thing started, I glance over my shoulder, put it in reverse and haul ass back to the highway. If I hit anyone on my way out of here, that's their fucking problem. Maybe the Bitch of Light can rub her body all over them and heal the wounds.

My thoughts go back to the shit I just witnessed almost immediately, and I tell myself that it doesn't have to happen today since I know where she is now.

Eventually all good things come to an end, and when I feel like the time is right, I'll come back.

As soon as the tires go from dirt to gravel, I straighten myself out in the seat, and shift the truck into drive.

Pressing down on the gas pedal, I crack my neck as I race back home.

The further away from this place—from *her*—I am, the better I'll feel.

And then I'll come back.

I'll make her remember Ichabod if nothing else.

Then the desert will flow with more than just junkie cactus water.

*See you soon, bitch.*

## About Yolanda Olson

Yolanda Olson is a *USA Today* bestselling and award-winning author. Born and raised in Bridgeport, CT where she currently resides, she usually spends her time watching her favorite channel, Investigation Discovery. Occasionally, she takes a break to write books and test the limits of her mind. Also an avid horror movie fan, she likes to incorporate dark elements into the majority of her books.

You can keep in touch with her on Facebook, Twitter, and Instagram.

**More books by Yolanda:**

Inferno: https://mybook.to/Inferno_

Death Blooms: http://mybook.to/deathblooms

Scavengers: http://mybook.to/scavengers

Sign up for Yolanda's newsletter here.

http://eepurl.com/gSvPo9

## About Jennifer Bene

Jennifer Bene is a *USA Today* bestselling author of dangerously sexy and deviously dark romance. From BDSM, to Suspense, Dark Romance, and Thrillers—she writes it all. Always delivering a twisty, spine-tingling journey with the promise of a happily-ever-after.

Don't miss a release! Sign up for the newsletter to get new book alerts (and a free welcome book) at:

http://jenniferbene.com/newsletter

You can find her online throughout social media with username @jbeneauthor and on her website:

www.jenniferbene.com

## Also by Jennifer Bene

### The Thalia Series (Dark Romance)

Security Binds Her *(Thalia Book 1)*

Striking a Balance *(Thalia Book 2)*

Salvaged by Love *(Thalia Book 3)*

Tying the Knot *(Thalia Book 4)*

The Thalia Series: The Complete Collection

### The Beth Series (Dark Romance)

Breaking Beth *(Beth Book 1)*

### Fragile Ties Series (Dark Romance)

Destruction *(Fragile Ties Book 1)*

Inheritance *(Fragile Ties Book 2)*

Redemption *(Fragile Ties Book 3)*

### Dangerous Games Series (Dark Mafia Romance)

Early Sins *(A Dangerous Games Prequel)*

Lethal Sin *(Dangerous Games Book 1)*

### Standalone Dark Romance

Imperfect Monster

Corrupt Desires

Deviant Attraction: A Dark and Dirty Collection

Reign of Ruin

Mesmer

Jasmine

Crazy Broken Love

**Standalone BDSM Ménage Romance**

The Invitation

Reunited

**Dark Suspense / Horror**

Burned: An Inferno World Novella

Scorched: A New Beginning

Noxious *(Anathema Book 1)*

Mephitic *(Anathema Book 2)*

Viperous *(Anathema Book 3)*

**Appearances in the Black Light Series (BDSM Romance)**

Black Light: Exposed *(Black Light Series Book 2)*

Black Light: Valentine Roulette *(Black Light Series Book 3)*

Black Light: Roulette Redux *(Black Light Series Book 7)*

Black Light: Celebrity Roulette *(Black Light Series Book 12)*

Black Light: Charmed *(Black Light Series Book 15)*

Black Light: Roulette War *(Black Light Series Book 16)*

Black Light: The Beginning *(Black Light Series Book 17.5)*

Black Light: Unbound *(Black Light Series Book 18)*

---

## Books Released As Cassandra Faye

### Daughters of Eltera Series (Dark Fantasy Romance)

Fae *(Daughters of Eltera Book 1)*

Tara *(Daughters of Eltera Book 2)*

### Standalone Paranormal Romance

Hunted *(The Dirty Heroes Collection Book 13)*

One Crazy Bite

Dangerous Magic